Vol

Winning

C. S. ADLER

Clarion Books • New York

Clarion Books
a Houghton Mifflin Company imprint
215 Park Avenue South, New York, NY 10003
Copyright © 1999 by Carole S. Adler

The text was set in 14-point Adobe Garamond.

Printed in the USA.

Library of Congress Cataloging-in-Publication Data

Adler, C. S. (Carole S.)
Winning / by C. S. Adler
p.   cm.
Summary: Vicky is thrilled to be on the eighth-grade tennis
team, until she realizes that her new playing partner Brenda is ruthless
about winning and will even cheat to do so.
ISBN 0-395-65017-8
[1. Tennis—Fiction. 2. Cheating—Fiction. 3. Winning and
losing—Fiction. 4. Sportsmanship—Fiction.] I. Title.
PZ7.A26145Wg   1999
[Fic]—dc21   98-51935
CIP
AC
QBP 10 9 8 7 6 5 4 3 2 1

With thanks to all of my tennis
buddies in Schenectady, Cape Cod,
and Tucson for the thousands of
hours of pleasure they've given me
on the courts

CHAPTER 1

The rhythmical thunk, thunk, thunk of the tennis ball against the backboard soothed Vicky the way waves hushing the shore always did. It was the look her eighth-grade English teacher had given her that had upset her, as if he couldn't believe that she was the sister of his favorite student.

"Your brother really could write," he'd said. "Well, I'm sure you'll put more effort into it next time, Vicky." And he had given her a C on the composition, even though she had done her best.

There! She slammed the ball at the backboard so hard that it returned too fast for her to get. She picked it up and slammed it again. She didn't mind that her friend Reggie was late. Hitting the tennis ball was making her feel better, as it usually did.

She stopped to wipe the sweat from her face with her hand, wishing she'd brought a towel.

Although it was late September and school had started weeks ago, Schenectady, New York, was in the middle of a heat wave. The trees were still heavy with green leaves, and it felt like mid-summer.

"You going to be using the backboard for long?" someone asked.

Vicky's heart leapt when she turned and saw Brenda Mack standing behind her with a tennis bag in her hand. Big, broad-hipped Brenda hit a tennis ball with a fierceness that made it zing past her opponents. Even in that long-ago summer after sixth grade when they had both begun taking tennis lessons, Brenda had been formidable on a court. Their teacher had called her gutsy, which Vicky knew she herself was not.

"I'm waiting for a friend," Vicky said. "She'll be here any minute." Taking a deep breath for courage, she asked, "Want to hit with me until she comes?"

Brenda looked at her doubtfully. "You started with the girls' tennis team last spring, didn't you? What made you drop out?"

"Well, first I pulled a ligament, and then I had pneumonia."

"Yeah, that'd do it. . . . I guess we could both use the backboard at the same time."

"Sure," Vicky said. She was embarrassed that

she'd asked Brenda to hit with her. Of course Brenda wouldn't want to risk pulling down her game by playing with someone who might be a lot weaker than she was.

"Sorry I'm late," Reggie called. Her pudgy body was stuffed into shorts and a T-shirt, and her everlastingly rosy cheeks seemed to bloom in her effort to hurry. "The dog got loose when I went home to change out of my school clothes. Mom and I had a heck of a time chasing him down."

Vicky smiled. Reggie's galumphing Saint Bernard always struck her as funny, but Reggie's parents took him seriously. They catered to that dog as if he were the most important member of the family. "So did he steal any of the neighbor kids' toys today?" Vicky teased.

"Nope. But we caught him with a Frisbee in his mouth and made him give it back," Reggie said.

Vicky picked up her balls, leaving the backboard for Brenda's sole use. The three girls nodded at each other as Vicky and Reggie moved off toward the nearest empty court.

Reggie held up an old wooden racket. "My mom dug this out of the garage. She got it from my grandmother. Will it do?"

"How about if I lend you mine?" Vicky said. "That'd be easier for you."

"Whatever you say." Reggie took Vicky's new lightweight Wilson and swung it. It had been a combination birthday and Christmas present, and it was Vicky's most prized possession.

"So where do I stand?" asked Reggie.

Gently Vicky placed her unathletic friend at midcourt. She had persuaded Reggie to try tennis by making her feel guilty. She'd pointed out that she, Vicky, was always at a disadvantage when they played board games, or when Reggie helped her with her homework, and even when Reggie's family invited her along on outings. "I'm not as smart as you, and not as rich either," Vicky had said.

Reggie had immediately gotten flustered and protested, "But you're pretty and I'm not, and you're good with physical stuff and I'm a klutz. Besides, it isn't my fault both my parents are doctors. And anyway, that doesn't make *me* rich."

She had flushed so hotly that Vicky hadn't had the heart to argue, even though she knew Reggie's parents were rich compared with her mother, who was supporting two children as a single parent on a teacher's salary. "Well, it wouldn't hurt you to hit some balls with me. You might even like it," Vicky had said.

Now, though, after forty minutes on the tennis court behind their school, Vicky could see that

Reggie would never like it. No matter how softly Vicky lobbed balls over the net, Reggie missed them. When she did manage to connect racket and ball, the results were disastrous. The ball either plunked into the net or sailed off the court at a bizarre angle.

"If you turn sideways to the ball when you hit it—" Vicky began.

"How about we just go back to doing the same things we've been doing together since fifth grade?" Reggie said.

"You hate this, huh?"

Reggie sighed. "My arm aches, and frankly, I don't really care if I ever hit the dumb ball."

The misery in her voice made Vicky relent. "Okay," she said, "we'll stop."

"It doesn't matter that much, does it?" Reggie asked. "You look so down. You didn't fail the remake in Spanish again, did you?" She sounded alarmed.

"No, I got a B. Thanks to your drilling me."

"So what's the matter?"

Vicky took a deep breath. She'd never convince Reggie that finding a tennis partner was really important to her. As for the other thing on her mind, Reggie would sympathize about the C on the composition all right, but Vicky didn't feel like telling her about it. She was sick of being consoled for having to work hard just to be average. "Never mind. Let's go to my house and have a snack," she said.

Reggie was so glad to leave the tennis court behind her that she didn't seem to notice Vicky's disappointment. Vicky told herself that she'd just have to go back to hitting against the backboard alone. It might not be much fun, but it was good practice.

Her brother, Derek, a high school junior, was on the phone in the kitchen when Vicky and Reggie walked in. Vicky was pretty in a slim, angular way, with flyaway black hair and narrow dark eyes. But Derek was handsome—not just handsome, but quick, mentally and physically. Everything came easily to him.

"Why did you eat all the cookies?" Vicky asked him when he had hung up. Only three were left in the package Mom had brought home just last night.

Derek smiled and winked at Reggie. "I know you girls worry too much about your figures to need more than one or two."

Reggie blushed and said nothing. She had probably seen Derek a few hundred times, but she'd never gotten over being tongue-tied in his presence.

Vicky frowned at him and went to pour a glass of skim milk for Reggie.

"So how's your tennis game?" Derek asked Reggie.

She dropped the wooden racket she was still carrying as if it were suddenly burning her hand. "Vicky's got to find herself another person to hit with. I'm hopeless."

"Didn't they start a girls' middle school tennis team last year?" Derek asked. "Why don't you try out for it, Vick?"

She didn't remind him that she *had* tried out last spring but had been forced to quit. These days he paid no attention to what was going on in her life and couldn't remember what she told him for more than five minutes. Now she said simply, "I want to try out for the team, but I'm not good enough yet. I need someone to practice with."

"You'll find someone," he said, without offering his services. Derek was good at tennis, although not interested enough in it to go out for his high school team. "Listen, Vick, can you do me a favor?"

"What?" she asked warily.

"Don't tell Mom you saw me home, okay? She wanted me to catch up on those science labs I missed, and I didn't get around to it."

"I don't lie to Mom. You know that," Vicky said.

"Okay, okay, just don't say anything. We can

leave it that I stopped by the house to pick up something. Just tell her I'm going to grab a bite with Carl at the mall."

"I thought you were broke."

"Right. Well, seems like my sweet little sister must have lent me enough for a slice of pizza."

"Derek! You took my money without asking me again?" Vicky was angry. "You're not fair. Just because I never tell on you—"

"Hey, you'll get it back. Come on, Sis. All you do is save your pennies. I'll tell you what, I'll pay you interest."

"Why don't you just pay me back?"

"I will." He smiled his winner's-circle smile at her. "Eat something. You're getting too skinny." He stood up and stretched his long, lean body. "See you, Reggie." As he took off out the back door, his predator's prideful stride and speed reminded Vicky of a cheetah.

"He's awful, isn't he?" Reggie said, as if she wanted to be convinced.

"He's going to drive Mom crazy," Vicky said. "He used to be her perfect child. But now he's wild. He used to be a halfway decent brother, too. At least when he was ten or eleven, he'd have played tennis with me once in a while. Now all he thinks about is himself."

"Are you jealous of him? I mean, because of how your mom treats him?"

"No, I don't think so," Vicky said. Her mother treated Derek as if he were something special—which he was.

"So what are you going to do?"

"About what?" Vicky asked.

"About tennis."

Her natural optimism returned, and Vicky said, "I'll find a partner. There has to be somebody in the eighth grade who wants to hit a tennis ball bad enough to play with me."

"It's really important to you, isn't it?" Reggie sounded as if that were hard to believe.

Vicky licked her lip. With some passion, she said, "Well, I need to win at something, Reggie."

"Yeah," Reggie said. "Sure. I'm sorry I can't help you. You know I'd like to. But tennis . . ."

"I know." Vicky managed a smile to reassure her friend.

"So, anyway, what do you want to do now?" Reggie had finished off two of the three cookies and her glass of milk. "Play cards? Play Boggle? Or we could go to my house and try that new game I got. Quarto? Unless you want to go over the Spanish vocabulary list."

"No. You can drill the new vocabulary into my

head the night before the next test. Any sooner and I'll forget." As for a board game, Vicky didn't feel like sitting still that long. "How about if I walk you over to your house, and then I can run back here before Mom gets home."

"That's four miles."

"Good exercise," Vicky said. She was looking forward to showing her mother the B she'd made on the makeup test. Mom had been upset about her flunking the first Spanish test of the term. Spanish was Vicky's worst subject, and neither her mother nor her brother could understand why. They claimed Spanish was easy. No doubt it was for them, Vicky thought.

The way she explained it to herself was that she must have inherited her father's brain. Not that she knew for sure how bright he'd been. He had left when Vicky was born, and they hadn't heard from him since. Mom refused to talk about him. All she'd say was that he'd been a tree trimmer for the telephone company. Probably he hadn't been much good at anything in school, either. He'd certainly flunked out of fatherhood. Vicky didn't spend much time wondering about him, though. She suspected he would have been as dazzled by his son's potential as Mom was.

Sometimes Vicky wished she'd been an only

child like Reggie, whose parents kept telling her how wonderful she was. "That's because they have nobody to compare me with," Reggie always said. But the remark was only meant to make Vicky feel better. Reggie's parents thought their daughter *was* wonderful. She was smart in school, and that was what they valued most.

As for Vicky, being a good kid, which was what she'd always tried to be, didn't impress anybody much, certainly not her mother. But she did have some talent for playing tennis. And she would get better at it. She'd be a winner on the court.

CHAPTER 2

By the time Vicky had run home from Reggie's, it was six o'clock and the sun was starting to set, taking the heat of the day with it. Vicky knew she didn't have time to shower before Mom got home from her weekly faculty meeting—not if she wanted to set the table and make the salad. Quickly she washed her face and hands at the kitchen sink. She was setting two places at the kitchen table when the garage door grumbled its way open. A moment later, Mom walked in with a slight frown that meant she was tired. Still, the mass of wavy black hair that Vicky had inherited was tightly bound in the French knot Mom favored for school, and she looked cool, as always.

"Hi, Mom. How was your day?"

"Oh, the usual. Only half the class did their homework, and I got stuck with lunchroom duty again. That new first-grade teacher is making the most of her pregnancy." Mom dropped her school case onto the stepstool and asked, "Where's your brother?"

"He said he was going to eat at the mall with Carl."

"Again? He never seems to stay home these days. I don't know how he can expect to get into a decent college if he spends all his time fooling around." Mom opened the refrigerator to survey prospects for their dinner. "Did he say anything about making up those science labs?"

"I barely spoke to him," Vicky said, hedging. "I played tennis with Reggie after school."

"Play, play, play," Mom said bitterly. "That's all you and your brother know. It's going to come as a shock to you both that life's more about work than having fun."

Vicky took the rebuke in silence. She felt sorry for her mother, for the way work had erased much of her prettiness and made her look older than her thirty-seven years.

"If it's just the two of us, we might as well finish up the leftover pasta primavera," Mom said. She pulled the covered Pyrex dish from the refrigerator shelf. "Derek didn't like it anyway."

"I got my Spanish makeup test back," Vicky said to cheer her up.

"Oh? I hope you managed to pass this time." Mom slid the dish into the microwave.

"I got a B."

"Well, good," Mom said with forced enthusiasm. "With the F, that'll average out to a C minus and you'll have a chance of passing—as long as Reggie doesn't get tired of tutoring you."

Vicky flushed. She had planned to show her mother the test, because the teacher had printed in the margin, "Congratulations on your fine improvement." Now she realized that Mom wouldn't be impressed. It would be like the time Vicky had raced home from fifth grade to show Mom the A she'd gotten for a poem she'd written about the sounds of the wind. "Very nice, Vicky," Mom had said, but then she'd added, "See, you can do it if you try."

Vicky did try. But whatever "it" was remained beyond her grasp. Derek had had an essay on video games published in the high school's literary magazine. *That* Mom had posted on the refrigerator for a year. Of course, Vicky's poem hadn't been published in anything, which could be why Mom had seen it as less valuable. But Vicky suspected that whatever she did would seem less valuable to her mother.

"You'd better take a shower before we eat, Vicky," Mom said with a disapproving glance. "You're all sweaty from tennis."

"I know. It was hot," Vicky said.

"And do something with that mop of yours while you're at it, will you?"

If Mom released her hair from its knot, it would spring out with the same energy Vicky's hair had. People told Vicky her hair was beautiful. Mom had never thought so. Neither was she satisfied with the slenderness they shared. "You're a skinny-ma-links like me," she'd point out, as if it were a fault.

Vicky showered and went back downstairs, where her mother had already dished out the pasta and put out a salad for each of them. "Do you have a lot of papers to mark tonight?" Vicky asked.

"The usual."

"I'll clean up the kitchen for you."

"Thanks. You're a good girl, Vicky." Mom's face became sweeter when she smiled. "How did Reggie do on the tennis court today?"

"Bad. She hates it."

"Well, you'll find someone else to play with. Did I tell you that one of the ladies from your grandmother's tennis league stopped me in the bank yesterday? She said you were a talented player."

"They were just happy to have someone take Grandma's place. Otherwise, they would have had to play Canadian doubles." At Mom's blank look,

Vicky explained, "That's what you play with three people. And they hate it."

"I miss her," Mom said sadly.

"Grandma? Me, too," Vicky said. Her grandmother had always made her feel good about herself. She had applauded everything Vicky did, as if Vicky were her brother's equal. Before the breast cancer Grandma had fought for years had finally defeated her in August, she had told Vicky, "I feel truly blessed to have a granddaughter like you."

The loss had been hard on Vicky, but still harder on Mom, who had been very attached to her mother.

• • • •

Vicky was in the living room struggling to translate a paragraph from Spanish into English when Derek clattered into the house that evening.

"How's it going, ladies?" he asked.

"Derek, were you at the mall all this time?" Mom asked, looking up from her papers.

"Just about, Mom. Why, would you rather have me painting graffiti or breaking windows somewhere?"

"I didn't realize those were the options. Did you do the lab makeups?"

"Didn't have time. I'll get to them. Don't sweat it."

Mom's voice got shrill. "Derek, don't you understand how important junior year is in terms of getting into a decent college? It doesn't matter how smart you are, if you don't perform well—"

He'd heard the lecture before. They all had it by heart. Now he cut her short with, "It could be I'll want to take a year off before I try college, Mom."

"Oh, no, you won't. I can't afford—"

Vicky picked up her notebook and text and ran upstairs to her bedroom. It was so small that she had to lie on her bed to do her homework, but that was better than listening to Mom sound off in frustration while Derek feinted and dodged whatever she threw at him. Vicky hated the way he tormented their mother. But neither did she like the way Mom humorlessly persisted in pushing Derek in the direction she believed best. Still, Vicky thought Mom's anxiety was reasonable. She had to be both mother and father to them, and she considered it her duty to see that her children succeeded. But Derek didn't have any excuse for his behavior. He just seemed to have turned mean in the past few years.

● ● ● ●

The dawn chorus of birds singing in the overgrown yard outside her bedroom window woke

Vicky. She'd fallen asleep without brushing her teeth, and she felt vaguely queasy. Normally her sky-blue closet of a bedroom, with its cornflower-and-daisy-printed bedspread, cradled her comfortably. It was a lighthearted, summery room, and Vicky considered herself basically a lighthearted, summery person. Derek was as unpredictable as spring, sometimes cold and rainy, sometimes bursting with promise. Mom was autumn, sad with the loss of things. But today—today Vicky decided she needed a tennis cure.

She used the bathroom as quietly as she could, so as not to wake anyone, and left a note on the kitchen table. *I'm off to hit some tennis balls before school. Have a good day, everbody. Love, Vicky.*

It was still dark under the big, old trees that had uprooted parts of the concrete sidewalk along the two blocks between her house and school. The streetlights had just gone off here in the old part of Schenectady, and the sunrise was pink over the top of the battered green backboard when she reached it. Vicky set her backpack against the fence and laid the cotton skirt and T-shirt she'd brought along to change into on top of it. She unsheathed her racket eagerly and began hitting forehands and backhands. She wanted to put more power in them, to hit the way Brenda did. When she'd hit a hundred or more, she moved closer to the backboard and tried volleying, but the ball came back so fast that she missed it more often than not.

She stopped to retrieve her balls and saw Brenda standing and watching her. "Hi," Vicky said in surprise.

"You're here again," Brenda said, stating the obvious.

"Did you want to use the backboard?" Vicky asked.

"No, that's all right. My partner should be coming along soon. I'll just practice my serves."

Brenda walked onto the court nearest the backboard. Vicky watched her out of the corner of her eye while she worked at hitting the ball just above the painted white band that represented the top of the net on a real court. Brenda's serves looked good, but a lot of them went long or wide. At least when it came to serving, Vicky told herself, she did as well as Brenda.

She waited to see if Brenda's partner was someone she knew. It might be Sandi. Open-faced, bouncy Sandi had been made captain of the eighth-grade girls' team. But Sandi didn't come. No one did, but it didn't seem to surprise Brenda.

At five to eight, Vicky picked up her balls and set off for her homeroom. *It wouldn't have hurt Brenda to hit with me for a few minutes,* she thought. But no doubt Brenda had seen her hitting the ball too softly. "Get your whole body into it, Vicky. Swing from the hips," the coach kept telling her last winter, and she'd started to do it before she pulled the ligament in her leg. Then this past summer Grandma's tennis ladies had taught her about doubles strategy and how to block balls at net. They had complimented her progress. But Brenda obviously didn't consider her worth playing with yet.

Vicky stowed her tennis gear in her locker, changed her clothes in the girls' room, and entered homeroom. She felt as down as when she'd awakened that morning. Brenda's snub had wiped out the high that usually came from hitting tennis balls. Running, swimming, and playing volleyball were just exercises Vicky did, as the gym teacher required. Only tennis turned her into a bird. Flying around a court returning balls exhilarated her as nothing else did. How was she going to find someone to play with? Her only hope was to keep practicing on the backboard until she improved enough to impress somebody—with luck, someone as good as Brenda or Sandi.

At lunchtime, Vicky found her way to the table closest to the cafeteria door, where she and Reggie usually sat.

"How'd you do on the map test?" Reggie asked after handing Vicky her bag of potato chips. Reggie was always on a diet and often griped good-naturedly that Vicky could eat what she wanted and stay reed-slim, while she starved herself and still her flesh plumped out her shiny skin.

"I got a B minus," Vicky said.

"Good. I told you you didn't have to worry."

"You got an A, didn't you?"

"Reggie gets an A in everything," said the sour-faced girl who sometimes joined them at their table for lack of any other companionship.

Reggie blushed. She knew it wasn't cool to be a serious student and to be grade-conscious, but her goal was to become a doctor like her parents. She had told Vicky that she wasn't about to let any social pressure to be average keep her from it. Average, Vicky had told herself. She herself ought to be the most popular girl in the school if being average was so desirable.

"How's your dog doing?" she asked, changing the subject.

"He had indigestion and threw up on Dad's new pants this morning."

"Was your father mad?"

"Dad? You know him. He just laughed. They want to know if you'd like to go to the flea market with us on Saturday."

"Sure," Vicky said. Reggie's family often shopped at the flea market and brought home antique kitchenware to decorate the brick wall of their kitchen. Once Vicky had found a paperweight there for her mother that Mom said was beautiful.

● ● ● ●

The afternoon went slowly because their lively English teacher was absent and the sub was strict and made the class work on their book reports as individuals instead of in pods, their regular teacher's favorite method. *Pods*—the word made Vicky feel like a sea creature.

Brenda was in Vicky's class. She sat with her friends in the back of the room and listened more than she talked. Her face was like a window that reflected what was outside rather than revealing what was inside. Vicky had no idea what the girl was really like.

Once Brenda caught Vicky watching her and gave an abbreviated smile. Vicky smiled back. Should she tell Brenda how much she admired her playing? Probably not. Brenda might suspect the compliment was a bribe. Well, Vicky *did* want something from her—she wanted Brenda to hit with her once in a while.

Putting punctuation marks into the worksheet paragraph, Vicky daydreamed that Sandi would come upon her working away at the backboard and comment on how well she was hitting. "Do you want to join the eighth-grade girls' tennis team, Vicky?"

"Oh, sure, that'd be great."

In truth, Sandi had been friendly to her in seventh grade when they were taking lessons and the gym teacher they'd had then had talked about forming a team. Sandi had even complimented her serve. Vicky fixed the run-on sentence in her paragraph and imagined herself winning a tennis match for the team.

"You're better than I thought," Sandi would say. "How about being my partner?"

"Why not?" Vicky would answer nonchalantly.

She smiled at herself. If only life were as good as a daydream!

CHAPTER 3

Reggie's parents' main reason for buying her the Saint Bernard puppy she had fallen in love with was that she'd be responsible for walking it, and that would force her to exercise. Reggie was firmly anti-exercise. She said it just made her tired and cranky. But walking Woof, her now full-grown woolly mammoth of a dog, was more than exercise—it was an ordeal.

On Wednesday after school, Vicky took her turn at being pulled on an erratic course from tree to fire hydrant to garbage can. Reggie's arms had started hurting after the first block. Woof looked back over his shoulder at Vicky when she took hold of the leash, his tongue hanging innocently and his brown eyes as sorrowful and sweet as ever. But as soon as she took her first step, he broke into a run.

Vicky raced along behind him, yelling, "Whoa!

Stop! Woof, you idiot, stop!" He finally halted when a car nearly took off his nose as he pulled Vicky across an intersection. Suddenly, in the exact middle of the road, he sat back on his haunches.

"Come on!" she told him. "You're blocking traffic."

Amiably he licked her chin. His tongue was broad. His breath was bad.

"Look," she said, "just because you're my best friend's dog doesn't make me like your kisses. Up, Woof. Up. Come on."

A car honked at them. Another car stopped, and a quavery-voiced old man told Vicky she'd better get her dog out of the street before they both got hit.

"I would if I could," Vicky told him, "but he won't budge."

The old man blew his horn, and Woof leaped up, reversed, and started galloping back toward home. Reggie met them halfway there. Woof stopped short to jump on her.

"This crazy dog of yours needs another go-round at obedience school," Vicky said.

"He's already been twice."

"But you're going to get killed trying to walk him."

"He's just frisky today because he's been alone too much. He's really a great dog, Vicky."

Vicky thought he was a great pest, but she didn't want to hurt Reggie by saying so. Reggie took the leash from her, and Woof walked peacefully back toward the big colonial house with the fenced-in back yard where he lived. His only detours were to lift his leg against the bases of two streetlights and three car bumpers, which Reggie tried to pull him away from without success. When they were in her family's spacious kitchen, she fed him a leftover hamburger patty followed by a cookie. Reggie didn't consider any meal complete without dessert.

"Want some chocolate mousse pie?" she asked Vicky.

"No thanks."

"You aren't hungry?"

"I'd like an apple, if you have one."

Reggie washed an apple and gave it to her. Then she sat down next to Vicky at the kitchen counter and served herself some of the chocolate mousse pie. Woof had slurped water all over the white tile floor and now flopped down on the rag rug near the door.

"Isn't he cute, though? Just look at how relaxed he is," Reggie said.

"Sort of like a bear rug," Vicky said.

"Oh, you. If he could play tennis, you'd think he was terrific."

Vicky laughed. "You're right. So you want to get out Quarto and I'll try it again?"

"You don't have to play if you don't want to," Reggie said. "We could just talk."

"What about?"

"I don't know. Life."

"Yours is perfect, isn't it, Reggie?" Vicky really wanted to know the answer. She had often wondered if Reggie realized how lucky she was to have her brains and two parents who adored her, plus the oversized pet whom she adored.

"I don't think so," Reggie said seriously. "If it was, I wouldn't feel lonely so much of the time."

The answer surprised Vicky. "Do you really? But I thought—I mean, your folks take you with them most places they go, and you have Woof, and . . ."

"I don't have a brother like you do. My parents aren't home much, and Woof can't talk." She took her empty plate to the sink and bent down to hug her dog, who groaned contentedly. "He's lovable, though. Actually," Reggie said, "I'm exaggerating. I'm only lonely in between seeing you and the folks and when Woof's not paying any attention to me."

"I don't get lonely much," Vicky said. "What I mostly get is mad at myself for not being better at things."

"I wonder how your brother feels," Reggie said. "I bet he's satisfied with his life."

"Derek's kind of rebellious right now. I don't know what he's feeling. We used to be close when he was younger and I was in elementary school. He was always telling me important stuff about life then, like how he handled problems with teachers and with other kids. He used to be so cool."

She stopped as the image of a younger, sweeter brother played in her head. "I remember once he made me stand in front of a mirror and practice acting brave for times when I was scared and I didn't want people to know. And you know what? It worked." Vicky shook her head. "If I was going to be lonely for anything, it'd be for how Derek was when we were little kids."

"You know why I like you?" Reggie asked.

"No. Why?"

"Because you're so honest. Also, I can trust you to be glad for me."

"About what?"

"Oh, you know," Reggie said. "Like when I get on the honor roll, you don't hate me for it. Or like when the folks bought Woof. You didn't even like him when he was a puppy, but you acted glad for me anyway."

"Why should I like a dog that scratches my shoulders when he jumps on me and slobbers all over my face?" Vicky asked. She hadn't forgotten how irrepressible Woof had been right from the beginning.

Reggie wrinkled her nose in pretend anger at Vicky's putdown of her dog. "Well, anyway, I feel like I can say anything to you," she said.

"And I can say anything to you." Vicky smiled. "Almost," she added truthfully, because she made an effort not to say whatever might hurt Reggie's feelings. "And besides, you're my only best friend."

Reggie blushed at this declaration. "I'll get Quarto," she said.

● ● ● ●

They played until five. At the end of the game, Vicky ran home. She found her mother already there and a bag from the discount store was on the kitchen table. "Tennis balls?" Vicky asked hopefully. She was down to her last can and she had told her mother she needed some more.

"Oh, no, Vicky. I'm sorry. I forgot. You should have written me a note to remind me. No, I got something for Derek. It's a CD-ROM for practicing for the SATs. They say it's excellent."

"And Derek wanted it?" Vicky asked in surprise as she pulled her hair back and tied it with a rubber band to keep her mother from complaining about its wildness.

"Well, he likes working on the computer, so I thought he would."

Derek liked playing *games* on the computer, but Vicky didn't correct her mother. She asked how her day had been and listened as Mom described a phone call from an irate parent. "I told her that it was not my responsibility to teach her child to value education, that was *her* job. She threatened to report me to the principal for my attitude, but it's the truth."

"He won't care if she does report you," Vicky said. "He thinks you're great, doesn't he?"

"The old principal did. This young man we have now hinted that he's been hearing a lot of complaints about me lately." Mom spoke anxiously, the frown deepening between her eyes. "I don't know. If I could afford to, I'd take a year's sabbatical. Well, maybe half a year."

"Can I do anything to help you, Mom?"

"No, dear. Don't worry. I'm not a basket case, just a little weary."

Her mother's voice was so soft that Vicky dared to put her arms around her and kiss her. "Want me to massage your forehead?" Vicky asked.

"Grandma used to do that."

"I know. She taught me how."

"Did she?" Mom closed her eyes, and Vicky rubbed her thumbs gently in the faint indentations on either side of her eyes. "That's nice," Mom said. "That's very nice, Vicky."

● ● ● ●

Derek thanked Mom for the CD-ROM, and after dinner he carried it with him up to the little alcove in the hall where they kept the family's computer. Passing him on her way to her room later, Vicky could tell by the sounds that he was playing some kind of combat game. "Derek," she said, "Mom just wants you to do well."

"I swear if she doesn't get off my case, I'm not going to college at all," he said without taking his eyes off the screen.

"Mothers are supposed to worry about their kids' futures. That's their job."

He turned from the colored objects whizzing before his eyes to look at her. "Nagging doesn't get anybody anywhere. It just makes the naggee—in this case, me—mad," he said. "And

I don't want to hear any echoes from you, little sister."

"Fine," she said and continued to her room.

She had tears in her eyes when she sat down on her bed and spread out her books to start on her homework. In her mind was the memory of how Derek had taught her to ride his two-wheeler the year he had outgrown it and she had inherited it. "You can do it, Vicky. You can do it," he'd called as he ran alongside her down the street holding the back of her seat to keep her upright. He'd been so patient and so reassuring. He'd taken her to her first grownup movie, too, using his allowance money. It had been a war story, and she hadn't liked it. He'd kept his arm around her comfortingly during the whole movie. She wondered what would make him go back to being her good big brother again.

Doing things for him didn't seem to work. She did his wash along with her own, and he never even thanked her. Once she cleaned his room for him when Mom got mad at him for not doing it. But all he had done in exchange for that favor was complain that she'd put his stuff in the wrong places. Maybe *she'd* be better off with a dog instead of a brother. She smiled to herself, thinking how little she'd like to be Woof's owner. Then she settled down to the reading she had to do for social studies.

• • • •

Vicky wore shorts and a T-shirt down to breakfast the next morning. She ate a bagel, then went to pick up her racket and balls in the hall. The racket was where she'd left it, but her last can of new balls was missing. A horn honked, and Vicky reached the front door just in time to see her brother getting into his friend's car with his tennis gear and a can of bright yellow Penn balls.

"Those are mine, Derek!" she yelled. "I bought them with my own money."

She gritted her teeth and groaned when he blew a raspberry at her out the open window of the old Toyota as it pulled out of the driveway.

She had promised herself new balls today. The ones she'd been using for practice were so dead they barely bounced. It wasn't fair. Derek supplemented the allowance Mom gave each of them with a neighborhood lawn maintenance business. He did well enough running it to hire younger kids to do the cutting and raking when he wasn't in the mood for drudge work. Vicky had no additional income, and her allowance barely covered birthday gifts and personal items like deodorant, which Mom expected her to buy for herself.

"What's all the yelling about?" Mom asked. She was dressed discreetly for school, with her hair pulled back tightly. She looked too severe to Vicky. What had happened to Mom's almond-eyed, willowy prettiness?

"Derek snatched my only new can of tennis balls," Vicky said.

Her mother smiled. "Sounds like quite the crime."

"It's not funny, Mom. He won't pay me back for them unless you make him."

"Remind me and I'll mention it to him at dinner," Mom said vaguely.

It was going on seven A.M. Vicky shouldered her backpack. She took a skirt and shirt to change into and made a dash for the tennis court. It could be worse, she told herself. He could have borrowed her racket. He was always mislaying his own, but fortunately the grip on hers was too small for him.

She was trying to whip her forehands against the backboard, thinking of Brenda and how to impress her, when she heard Brenda say, "You again! Are you here every day?"

"I probably will be. Unless it rains," Vicky said.

"Well, good for you." Brenda gave Vicky the thumbs-up sign and continued to the courts.

Another girl carrying a racket came running up, yelling, "I'm here, Brenda! I'm here." It was Sandi, as perky as ever.

"Sandi—hi," Vicky called out, hoping the team captain would remember her.

"Vicky? Vicky Baylor?" the pug-nosed girl stopped to ask.

"Yes. I haven't seen you around this fall, Sandi. Have you been gone?"

"Yeah, I've been with my dad, out west. But now I'm back until next summer."

Vicky remembered hearing that Sandi's parents had gotten divorced. She didn't know what to say, so she said nothing.

"Are you playing tennis this year?" Sandi asked.

"I want to."

"Good. Maybe you can come out and practice with the team. We'll be here before school sometimes, and always on Fridays."

"Thanks, that'd be great," Vicky said eagerly.

Sandi reached her partner, who was waiting for her at the gate to the first court. Something in Brenda's expression seemed to make her amend her invitation. "I mean, if we're short a player, you can step in," Sandi said over her shoulder at

Vicky. "Sometimes we get an uneven number, you know?"

"Fine with me," Vicky said.

Sandi smiled her freckle-faced, friendly smile. "See you, then," she said and began warming up at the net with Brenda.

Tomorrow, Vicky promised herself, she'd be so terrific on the court that Brenda would beg to hit with her. The momentary surge of confidence made Vicky smile at herself. She practiced hitting just above the painted white line on the backboard. Low over the net was good playing even if the hit was soft, according to Grandma's buddies. And for doubles, it was important to hit consistently, Vicky reassured herself. Still, she was afraid that Brenda might never be impressed with such an understated style of play.

Average—was she just average and ordinary at tennis, as she was in school and at everything else in life? Vicky whacked the ball with all her strength for an answer. It sailed over the top of the backboard and disappeared. She sighed and set out to find it.

CHAPTER 4

Thursday at lunch Reggie reminded Vicky that she'd agreed to go to the flea market on Saturday. "My mother said we'll pick you up around nine. It doesn't open until ten, but Mom likes to get there before the good stuff gets picked over," Reggie said.

"Fine with me," Vicky said, without giving the outing much thought.

That afternoon she got a compliment from the art teacher on her whimsical papier-mâché bird. She went home feeling good enough to take on Derek herself, without waiting for Mom.

"It's not fair to steal my balls when it's so easy for you to get your own, Derek."

He put down the container from which he was gulping juice and said, "I didn't know those were your balls when I took them. Sorry."

She grimaced. He *had* known they were hers.

Derek could lie without compunction when it was convenient. She didn't understand how he could do it so smoothly. She couldn't make herself lie, except to avoid hurting someone.

"Well, are you going to replace them?"

"Yeah, sure. When I get a chance."

"I need some for tomorrow. At least give me back the ones you used."

"Can't. I left them on the high school tennis court."

"But they were brand-new."

"Not after we slammed them around the court for an hour."

"Derek, I don't have any balls left that bounce."

"So use your partner's. I take it you've found someone to play with, since you're having such a hissy fit about balls."

"I hate you," she said. "You're so mean."

"I know," he said. "I'm a beast. Sorry, little sister." He patted her head as if she were a small child.

She pulled away from him and ran up to her room. When they were young, she and Derek had shared a room. Then Mom had used the third bedroom as her study. Now that the study had become Vicky's bedroom, she had a sanctuary to escape to. That was something to be grateful for, she told herself as she threw herself onto her bed. But she didn't feel grateful, just angry.

How could she show up at tennis practice tomorrow morning without decent balls to contribute? As much as she hated to ask Mom to drive her to the discount store for new ones, she'd better do it.

As it turned out, Mom wasn't hard to persuade. She said she needed to pick up a few things herself and was sorry she'd forgotten to get balls for Vicky earlier in the week.

When they were settled into the cozy confines of the front seat of the car, Vicky asked, "Mom, do you think Derek has changed a lot?"

Her mother sighed and admitted, "He's certainly become difficult to live with, hasn't he? He seems to be at a stage when boys need to assert their independence. At least, that's what the adolescent psychology books tell me."

"Well, he's changed a lot toward me, too," Vicky said. "And I don't see what that has to do with his independence."

"How do you mean?"

"He used to act as if he liked me. Now he doesn't."

"Nonsense, Vicky. Of course your brother likes you. He's just going through a difficult phase."

Vicky wondered if Mom had gotten that from a

book, too. She certainly couldn't know how brothers and sisters behaved to each other from personal experience, because she'd been an only child.

"Mom, do you think I'm pretty?" Vicky asked, just to see what her mother would answer.

"Of course you're pretty," Mom said. But she spoiled the compliment by adding, "Not that that's so important in life. It's what you can do, not what you look like, that matters."

"Hmm," Vicky said. For a panicky moment she couldn't think of anything that she could do really well. Hit a tennis ball, she reminded herself finally. She could do that.

When they got back home, Vicky thanked her mother for the balls and carried them off to her bedroom. She tucked them under her pillow for safekeeping. Who knew how far her brother would go to make her life miserable in his present "phase"?

● ● ● ●

True to her word, Sandi included Vicky in tennis practice Friday morning. Five team members showed up that day. Including Vicky, that made enough for one court of doubles and one of singles. She played singles with a tall, thin girl named Sonja who never came to net.

"You're all over the place," Sonja said after she had

lost the first set to Vicky, three games to six. Her complaining tone of voice made Vicky doubt she'd been given a compliment, so she simply smiled.

"How'd it go?" Sandi asked when it was time to leave the courts for class.

"Oh, she beat me," Sonja said airily. "I told you I'm better at doubles. And besides, I'm not feeling all that well today. I just got my period."

Sandi winked at Vicky. "Good practice for everybody, anyway," she said. "Will you come out again, Vicky?"

"Oh, yes. I really need people to hit with."

"You and Brenda should get together. She's always looking to hit with someone," Sandi said.

Vicky was sure that Brenda had heard, but she walked off toward school with her teammates, pretending she hadn't.

"You've improved a lot since last year," Sandi said to Vicky, possibly to make up for Brenda's snub. "At least, from what I've seen so far."

"Thanks," Vicky said. She hoped Brenda wouldn't veto it if Sandi ever asked her to join the team. Judging by the number of girls who'd attended the practice, they could use another member. She'd just keep hitting balls against the backboard, and maybe, with luck, she'd wear down Brenda's resistance.

At lunch Vicky eyed the table where the team sat. She recognized Sandi and Brenda and Sonja, plus another girl whose name she couldn't remember.

"Did you hear a word I said?" Reggie asked her.

"Hmm?"

"You didn't, did you? I was telling you about how Woof howled last night and I had to take him up to my bedroom to keep him quiet."

"Uh-huh," Vicky said, dutifully turning her attention to her friend.

"So what did he do then?" Reggie quizzed her with narrowed eyes.

"I don't know," Vicky said.

"Like I told you, he peed on my sneakers. Vicky, what's the matter with you?"

"Nothing. I just was trying to remember someone's name."

"You remember that we're going to the flea market tomorrow, don't you?"

"Sure. When did you say you'd pick me up?" She thought if she got up really early, she might get in an hour of practice on the backboard beforehand.

• • • •

That night Mom caught Derek playing his computer game and discovered he hadn't even taken the CD-ROM she'd bought him out of its package.

"Derek, do you want to spend your life digging ditches?"

"Hey, Mom, let's not get so dramatic. I'll do okay on the SATs."

"Okay is not good enough. You've got the brains to get into a good college, and that's what I expect from you."

"How about picking on your daughter for a change, huh, Mom? All she cares about is tennis. Do you approve of that?"

"Vicky does her homework every night. Do you?"

"Not always. I guess I'm not an overachiever like you, Mom. I must take after my father."

"You do not!" Mom yelled. "You may look like him, but you've got brains, and not to use them is sinful, Derek, especially since—"

Vicky closed the door to her room to muffle their argument. She didn't know how Derek could stand being yelled at so often. Just listening to Mom harass him made Vicky's nerves skitter about like scared mice. She slipped the weekly Spanish test out of her notebook and looked at it for the first time. She hadn't dared to look at it in class, for fear she'd burst into tears in public if she'd failed again. The test was marked with a C. Well, at least she'd passed. She sighed deeply and decided to do her math worksheets so that she wouldn't have to think about them over the weekend.

The phone rang just as she finished. "It's for you, Vicky," Mom called from downstairs.

"So how did you make out on your Spanish?" Reggie asked.

"I passed."

"*Bueno.* See you tomorrow. Sleep well."

"You, too," Vicky said. It touched her that Reggie had cared enough to ask.

• • • •

The rain streaming down her windowpane mocked Vicky's plan for Saturday morning. She dressed for tennis anyway and went to the kitchen for a bowl of cereal at seven. It might stop before long, and she could get in some practice even if the courts were a little wet.

Vicky went through the kitchen door into the sandbox-size back yard. It was jammed with overgrown bushes and a detached garage with a broken window where spiderwebs grew amid stored bikes and gardening equipment. Drizzle, just drizzle, she told herself.

Swinging her sheathed racket, Vicky walked past yards full of glistening crayon-colored toy cars and swings and slides. She was glad that young families lived in her neighborhood. Squealing preschoolers enjoying themselves in their busy way made her smile. She wondered if she and Derek had rolled around in the grass and giggled when they were little. What she recalled was following him around adoringly whenever he let her. That had ended when he reached his teens and stopped trying to please Mom.

Not a soul was in sight at the school tennis courts, and the fuzzy gray air under the dripping trees made for a funereal atmosphere. Vicky was about to open the new can of balls when a voice said, "Don't open a new can in this weather. I've got some old balls we can hit with."

It was Brenda.

Vicky felt as if the sun had suddenly come out. "Great," she said, and followed Brenda's broad back to the nearest court.

"Let's start up at net," Brenda said.

That went well. Brenda missed often enough to keep Vicky from feeling outclassed.

"You like singles or doubles best?" Brenda asked.

"Either's fine. I just like to play."

"I like doubles," Brenda said. "Let's move back."

They practiced forehand and then backhand ground strokes from the baseline. "You hit too softly," Brenda observed. "If you followed through, you'd get more power."

Vicky tried, but her shots kept landing in mid-court instead of at the baseline. "I wish I could hit like you," she said. "You can even hit winners from the baseline."

"Yeah, but you're faster than me, so you get to everything," Brenda said to Vicky's delight. "Let's try serving."

Brenda complimented Vicky on her serving and asked if she could control where she placed the ball.

"I think so. Pretty much." Vicky proved it by calling out where she was planning to hit the ball and mostly getting it there.

They stopped to take a drink of water, and Brenda said, "I'm going to have to stop soon. My mother's taking me shopping for my brother's birthday."

"I have a brother, too," Vicky said. "Mine's three years older than me."

"Mine's thirteen years older than me," Brenda said. "He's going to be twenty-six tomorrow."

"And that's all you have, just a brother?"

"And a mother and father," Brenda said. "How about you?"

"Brother and mother is all."

Brenda's straight brown hair hung in wet strands

around her full face. She said, "You're lucky you have a such great head of hair."

Vicky touched her head and could feel that her hair had frizzed up into a great dark halo from the dampness. "You really like it?"

"Uh-huh," Brenda said. "Let's practice some down-the-line shots."

A few minutes later Brenda looked at her watch and said, "Oops. I've got to go."

Vicky checked her watch. She could hardly believe they'd been hitting for an hour and a half, and now she was late.

"Want to try this again before school Monday?" Brenda asked as she gathered her belongings.

"Sure," Vicky said gladly. Her grin lasted through the whole run home.

Reggie's mother's important-looking silvery gray town car was waiting in her driveway. "Sorry," Vicky said. "Have you been waiting long?"

"Just a few minutes," Reggie's mother said.

Vicky dumped her tennis gear inside the house, yelled to her mother that she was leaving and, without stopping to change her clothes, slid onto the plush leather back seat of the car next to Reggie. Again Vicky apologized for making them wait. Reggie's mother said it was no problem. But Reggie was frowning.

"How come you look so happy?" Reggie asked. When Vicky told her, Reggie raised an eyebrow. "So what's so wonderful—that she's willing to hit with you? You're a good player, aren't you?"

"Not as good as she is," Vicky said.

Reggie sniffed. She couldn't understand because she didn't care about tennis.

The flea market was full of junk that morning. None of them found anything they wanted to buy. Reggie picked up a music box, but her mother said it sounded tinny. "Don't you think so, Vicky?" she asked.

"I'm not very musical," Vicky said.

Reggie put the box down and didn't answer when her mother asked if they wanted to stop somewhere for a soda. Vicky looked at Reggie to see what she wanted, but her friend wouldn't meet her eyes. It was getting late. "I probably should just go home," Vicky said.

They got into the car in silence, and Reggie still wasn't talking when they started onto the highway. "What's wrong?" Vicky asked her.

"Nothing," Reggie said. "I'm sorry I took you away from your tennis for this. I guess it wasn't much fun for you."

"Sure it was," Vicky said. But Reggie just eyed her sulkily.

At Vicky's house, she thanked Reggie's mother politely and said, "See you Monday, Reggie."

Reggie nodded and said accusingly, "Don't forget the annual book fair's next Friday, and I volunteered us both to help, like we always do."

"Sure, no problem," Vicky said. She couldn't imagine what she had done wrong.

CHAPTER 5

At practice on Monday, an even number of team members showed up, so Vicky worked alone at the backboard. She saw Mr. Finn, the new gym teacher, arrive, frowning and prissy-faced as usual. "Listen up," he commanded the four girls who were practicing at net. They gathered around him, and he asked Sandi where the rest of her team was.

"Not everybody shows up for every practice," she told him. "Maybe if they knew they'd get some coaching—"

"Yeah, well, you girls'll have to practice on your own this fall, because I don't have five minutes to spare. I've got soccer and cross-country and then basketball. Means I'm in three places at once already. But I'll get to you before the official season starts next spring. I promise."

"We have matches this fall, Mr. Finn," Sandi said.

"I know, I know, but the fall games, they're just so you can size up your opponents for the spring. You've got a match this Friday, and I'll give you the rest of your fall schedule as soon as I can get it. You just keep hitting the balls as best you can, okay?"

"We were told someone would coach us," Sandi said calmly.

"And someone will. Someone will when I find parents to help me who know what they're doing. Meanwhile, you do your best and so will I, okay?"

Sandi shrugged. "Okay, I guess," she said.

Mr. Finn bustled off like a tightly wound-up toy. After a few minutes of griping about being neglected because they were a new team and because they were girls, the team members began a doubles game. Five minutes into that, a girl whom Vicky didn't know tripped and had to be helped to the nurse's office. That broke up the practice session altogether.

Later, Sandi stopped Vicky in the hall to tell her that the girl had broken her ankle and to ask, "Vicky, could you play in her place if we need you in our match this coming Friday?"

"I guess so," Vicky managed to say, although her heart had stopped beating for a second.

"Good. We're allowed to use subs, since this isn't the official season. So that'll work."

Frozen with apprehension, Vicky sat through an assembly on the environment and how it was the responsibility of each person not to waste water, pollute the air, or poison the earth. The messages barely reached her. She felt like a faucet running first hot and then cold. The hot was the possibility of playing on the team. The cold was fear that she wasn't good enough to handle it.

"You okay?" Reggie asked her at lunch. She appeared to have gotten over her dark mood of Saturday.

"I think so," Vicky said. "Why are you asking?"

"You look funny. As if you're off somewhere."

"Sandi asked me to play in a match this coming Friday. I guess I'm scared. I mean, I'm thrilled—but scared, you know?"

"Not exactly. It's just a game, isn't it?"

"Reggie, this matters to me." It suddenly seemed important that her best friend understand.

"Okay, sure. I get it," Reggie said. "You'll be too busy to help set up for the book fair on Friday then, huh?"

"On Friday . . . I told you," Vicky repeated slowly, "I've got a chance to play for the eighth-grade girls' tennis team. I can't miss that, Reggie." She couldn't spell it out any more clearly.

"Right. Well, I guess I can haul books without your help." Reggie finished her pizza in silence.

She's mad at me again, Vicky thought. But why? Hurt by Reggie's lack of sympathy, she finished her tuna fish sandwich in silence. Then, relenting, she offered Reggie her cookie.

"I told you. I'm on a diet," Reggie said irritably.

If Reggie had told her any such thing, Vicky hadn't heard it. But she wasn't about to say that and have Reggie accuse her of not paying attention again. Their silence carried them through the rest of the lunch period.

• • • •

That night, doing her homework in the living room, Vicky had to listen to Derek battling with Mom in the kitchen about using her car.

"You said I could use it when I passed driver's ed. Well, I passed it last summer and you've barely let me touch the car," Derek complained.

"The agreement was you were going to pay for that taillight you broke before you could use my car again. Do you have the money, Derek?" Mom asked.

"I'm good for it. Carl had to put on some new

shocks, and I paid for them because he didn't have a dime. I figured, you know, I've been letting him drive me everyplace, so I owe him."

"I thought you were earning plenty from your lawn business."

"I am, but I've got expenses, Mom."

"Well, so do I, Derek, and I'd like you to pay for that taillight as you promised."

"If it was Vicky, you wouldn't expect her to pay."

"Vicky's not as old as you are." Mom sounded battle-weary.

"That's not the point."

"Then what *is* the point, Derek? Do you think I treat you unfairly?"

"Sometimes," he said.

Their fighting kept Vicky from concentrating. She wished she could turn them off like a TV or a radio. She wished they would stop sparring with each other all the time. Their conflict had turned her into a bystander in her own family. Finally, when it didn't seem they were going to stop, she picked up her books and papers and went upstairs to her room.

● ● ● ●

It turned out that Sonja was to be Vicky's partner in the after-school match that Friday. They had been lab partners once, and they hadn't gotten along any better then than the time they'd played singles against each other. Sonja's long, thin face showed neither dismay nor pleasure as Sandi explained to her that Vicky was filling in for the girl who'd broken her ankle.

"I think you two will be good together," Sandi assured Sonja, who nodded without enthusiasm. "Anyway, I'll put you on third court and we'll see how it goes."

Sonja focused her muddy hazel eyes on Vicky. "Do you want forehand or backhand?"

"Well, my forehand's a little better than my backhand," Vicky said.

"I usually play forehand," Sonja said. She sounded discouraged.

"Fine," Vicky said quickly. "I'll take backhand, then."

They warmed up with two of their own team members, Kelly, who was freckled and fierce, and her overweight partner, Bette. Bette looked as if she'd have trouble moving, but she was actually the faster of the two. And she was the only one to give Vicky a smile.

"I don't remember you from last year. Are you new?" Bette asked her.

"No, I was here for most of last year, but I

couldn't play tennis in the spring." Vicky explained what had happened to her.

"Too bad," Bette said. "So you haven't played much?"

"Oh, I played three or four times a week all summer." Vicky hoped Bette wouldn't ask with whom.

"They say this ninth-grade team we're playing today is tough," Kelly said.

"They are," Bette agreed. "But Sandi said not to worry. We're out to get experience, and nobody expects us to beat a high school team."

Vicky breathed a sigh of relief. "I'm glad there's no pressure to win," she said.

"Well, we should *try* to win," Sonja said, as if Vicky might be planning not to.

"Sure, we'll try," Bette said. "Come on. Let's play."

Bette and Kelly moved well together. Both of them came to net, and Kelly put the ball away with authority. Vicky was impressed with their teamwork. Meanwhile, Sonja stationed herself on the service line and moved neither forward nor back. In fact, she barely moved at all. When an easy ball, like a floater, came her way, she returned it at an angle and smiled with satisfaction at her accomplishment. Meanwhile, Vicky was left to run down balls on the other three quarters of the court.

Twice Bette told Vicky, "Great get." The compliments tamed the nervousness that was making Vicky rush some balls and hit them into the net.

When it was time for their match to begin, the four of them wished each other good luck, and Bette and Kelly left the court. The girls from the high school team who took their places were a tough-looking pair. They were tall, big-boned, and some thirty pounds heavier than Vicky or Sonja. Both ninth-graders were blondes with short haircuts.

"They could be twins," Vicky whispered to Sonja.

Sonja was frowning as glumly as if she were already defeated. "They *are* twins," she muttered. "They shouldn't be on third court. They're too good."

The twins won the spin and elected to serve. Sonja missed the first serve, which dropped at her feet. When it was Vicky's turn to receive serve, she got the ball back, but one of the blondes whacked it down the middle and Sonja let it go by. At the last second, Vicky tried for it and missed. They lost the first three games without making a point. Then Vicky managed to win a game with her serve. That didn't cheer Sonja up any. She seemed to have grown roots on the service line. Vicky ran around her and behind her to return balls, but she wasn't a strong enough player to put the ball away, and the ninth-graders hardly ever missed.

"Nice game," one sister said to Vicky when the match was over in record time. The score was 6–1, 6–0.

"Sorry we didn't give you better competition," Vicky said.

The twins smiled, a little smugly, as if they'd expected the easy win.

The four of them went outside the chain-link fence to watch the matches still in progress on the other courts.

"Sorry, Sonja," Vicky said to her partner. "That was a disaster."

Sonja shrugged. "Oh, well," she said airily. "You're new. Sandi can't expect much when we've never played together before."

Or when you don't go after the balls, Vicky thought, but she didn't say it. Their team lost every match except for Sandi and Brenda's on first court. That went to a third set. Sandi and Brenda won it in a tie-breaker that took so long that

Vicky and Sonja were the only team members who stayed to watch them win.

Sandi seemed exhilarated coming off the court. She and Brenda accepted congratulations, and then she asked Sonja, "So how did you guys do?"

"We're no good together. I need somebody who can keep them back from the net for me."

"Oh?" Sandi looked at Vicky. "How did you think you played, Vicky?"

"Not as well as I can, I guess." It was her first time ever in competition, but she didn't offer that as an excuse.

"Hmm. You probably need more practice," Sandi said. "Keep coming out with the team, why don't you?"

"Thanks, I will," Vicky said.

"And thanks for filling in for us," Sandi said.

Vicky saw Brenda watching her. She wondered if Brenda could see how bad she felt. No matter. She understood now that she wasn't anywhere near good enough to be invited to be on the team, much less to play with Brenda.

On her way home, Vicky tried to puzzle out how she could have played better and decided that what she needed was coaching from a pro. While her mother was molding hamburgers for dinner, Vicky asked hesitantly, "Mom, would you let me take some tennis lessons? I really need them."

Mom frowned at her. "Tennis lessons? Vicky, tennis is a frill. What you need is to improve in school subjects like Spanish. I'd be willing to scrounge up some money for tutoring in that, because it's important to your future."

"Thanks, but no thanks," Vicky said quickly. "I've got Reggie for Spanish." Or she had had Reggie, until lately.

• • • •

A week passed. Much of it Vicky spent hitting balls against the backboard in the hope that repetition would somehow improve her game. Brenda showed up to hit with her only once. As for Reggie, she remained distant, and when Vicky asked her what was wrong, she said only, "Well, you're so busy with tennis."

"I don't play at night," Vicky said.

"No? You don't call me then either, like you used to."

Vicky couldn't think of an answer to that.

"It's okay," Reggie said in an aggrieved tone of voice that frustrated Vicky. "I understand."

Vicky didn't think she did, but she wasn't about

to get on her knees and beg for Reggie's friendship. Still, it upset her that things had gotten so sour between them.

Her faithful appearance at the courts was being noticed by some team members. They greeted her cheerily by name, and Bette told her, "Way to go, Vicky. You're looking good." The following week Sandi asked her if she'd like to be on the team as a substitute until the girl with the broken ankle came back. They had tried out other girls, but apparently none had been better than Vicky.

Vicky was thrilled. "Fine," she said. "Thanks."

On a crisp Saturday when every leaf and grass blade sparkled, Vicky arrived at the backboard and found Brenda already there.

"I figured you'd come," Brenda said. "You live on these courts."

"So do you. The difference is, your game shows it."

"You're not so bad. Better than that partner you had, anyway. Sonja's a slug on court."

Vicky had it on the tip of her tongue to politely defend Sonja's playing, but she didn't. Sonja hadn't given her any credit, so she didn't deserve any in return. "Thanks," Vicky said simply.

Brenda suggested they hit for a while. When

they'd finished an hour of drills involving net play and cross-courts and overheads, she said, "Want to come over to my house? I've got a tape on doubles strategy that I borrowed from the library. It's pretty good."

"Sounds great," Vicky said. She'd planned to call Reggie and invite her over for the afternoon, but that could wait. This was an opportunity that might not come again.

"So," Brenda said as they began walking away from the school grounds, "what do you like to do besides tennis?"

"Oh, I like everything."

"Pain and suffering?"

"No." Vicky laughed, embarrassed that she couldn't offer anything impressive. "You know. I like doing handicrafts. Like I used to be big on making my own paper dolls and designing outfits for them, and I spent time last year learning origami. I decorated a Christmas tree in the children's ward at the hospital with them. I like art in general, but I'm not that talented."

"So how come you spend so much time on tennis?"

"I don't know. It's the first sport I've ever really enjoyed."

"Yeah. Me, too. I love tennis," Brenda said.

They were passing older houses whose open garages bulged with bicycles and lawn equipment, leaving no room for the cars they'd been intended to shelter. Next came a new development of four- and five-bedroom homes with two-car garages, each house on a large landscaped lot. No sidewalks here, and no streetlights, just individual lampposts at each driveway. The last house on the curved street they turned into was a large red-brick colonial with a wing over the garage. "This is where I live," Brenda said.

"It's beautiful," Vicky replied.

Brenda raised an eyebrow. "You think so?"

Vicky laughed. "Well, to me it is. My house could fit in your garage."

"Do you always put yourself down?" Brenda asked.

"I don't think so. Do I?"

"Yeah, you do. You're never going to win at tennis if you sell yourself short, Vicky."

"I didn't know I was selling myself short."

"Well, you are."

Vicky thought about it. "You think if you act sure of yourself, it makes you that way?"

"It helps."

"Maybe you're right," Vicky said. "I'll keep that in mind."

"You know," Brenda said, "I told Sandi that I thought you'd be good on the team because you try so hard."

"You *did?*"

Brenda nodded.

"Thanks," Vicky said with real gratitude.

"That's okay. Just remember, you've got to want to win."

"Right," Vicky said. "Okay." She was so glad to have gained Brenda's respect that she'd have promised anything at that moment.

"My folks work on Saturdays. Dad's got a plumbing supply business, and he's always there," Brenda said as they entered the spacious center hallway. It had a handsome curved staircase that led to an upper floor. "Mom is a volunteer at the hospital. But my brother Tom'll be home."

Tom was sitting at a computer in a room off the hall that seemed to have been turned into an office. He had Brenda's dark brown eyes and hair, but where she was chunky, he was fat. Face, arms, the body that filled and overflowed the office chair, all were oversized.

"Hi," Tom said to Vicky. "She let you beat her?" His smile was beautiful.

"What?" Vicky asked, startled. Then she realized

she was holding a tennis racket and so was Brenda. "She couldn't let me beat her," Vicky said. "She's too much better than me."

"There you go again," Brenda noted. And she told her brother, "Vicky's fast and her serve's good. I figure she's got potential. How did you do with your old ladies, Tom?"

"Fine," he said. "They think I'm a giant Sir Galahad. Too bad I can't make a full-time job out of running errands for them."

"Maybe you can," Brenda said.

"Nah. Most of them don't have any money. I can't even charge them. Besides, there's wear and tear on Dad's car, and gas costs."

"You know what Mrs. G said? She said you ought to go to seminary and become a minister," Brenda said. "Then you'd get paid for helping people."

"Can't," Tom said. "They make those student desks too small." He laughed, but Brenda didn't.

"Come on up to my room and I'll play the videotape for you," Brenda said to Vicky.

Brenda's room was pretty, with roses and violets printed on the wallpaper and matching drapes. She had her own TV and VCR, as well as an electronic keyboard.

"Do you play?" Vicky asked.

"I use it for practice. We have a grand piano in the living room."

"Oh." Vicky was impressed. She sat down in an upholstered armchair while Brenda popped in the tape. "Your brother seems very nice," Vicky said.

"Yeah, Tom's a honey, but he's driving my parents nuts. He's twenty-six years old, a college dropout, and all he does is sit around the house and eat."

"You said . . . you asked him about his job?" Vicky questioned.

"Right. Well, that's just started, and it's volunteer. Besides, he'll probably flub it, the way he's flubbed everything the folks have set up for him."

"Is he always nice to you?"

"Tom doesn't know how to be anything but nice."

"I think I'd trade him for my brother," Vicky said.

"Really?" Brenda looked interested. "Your brother's a beast?"

Vicky bit her lip. "Not really." She was embarrassed that she'd complained about her family to someone who wasn't yet a friend. "But he can be annoying," she said, and Brenda didn't push it.

It occurred to Vicky on the way home that she might be making another friend who had everything. Well, she wasn't exactly deprived, Vicky told herself. And what did she have that was special? Potential, Vicky told herself humorously. She had potential.

CHAPTER 6

It was forty-five degrees out, a chilly October morning for upstate New York. To make it worse, a strong breeze was blowing crimson and gold leaves off the sugar maples around the tennis courts. Brenda sent up a high lob, Vicky's least favorite shot. She ran back toward the baseline, turned, and hit the return beyond the reach of Brenda's backhand.

"Hey, not bad!" Brenda said. "You're getting better at those."

The words were encouraging, but Vicky knew her overheads were still weak. At Brenda's suggestion, she tried turning her shoulder to the ball more on the next one. Brenda seemed to be tutoring her lately, passing along tips she'd learned from her tennis coaches. That was fine with Vicky. She was happy to take instruction as long as Brenda was willing to practice regularly with her.

As for Sandi, she had begun treating Vicky like a regular team member, informing her of matches and practices, even adding her name and phone number to the roster. Sandi had scheduled her for another match this coming Friday. Vicky didn't know who her partner would be, but she'd played with most of her teammates and was comfortable with everyone but Sonja. Sonja was still giving herself credit for being a good player solely on the basis of her midcourt volleying ability. At least, Vicky told herself, she knew she was a weaker player than anybody else on the team, except possibly Sonja. But she planned to work hard at improving.

"So how are you on strange foods?" Brenda asked her when they stopped to take off one of the layers they'd put on against the cold. Vicky had both a sweater and a vest under her warm-up jacket.

"I'll try anything once," Vicky said.

"Yeah? Thin people are usually picky, but if you're not, Tom's making dinner a week from Sunday, and you're invited. Beware. He likes to experiment."

"That sounds like fun," Vicky said.

"Come around six. Tom likes you. He says you're sweet and pretty—which is not how he describes me."

"I thought you and he got along so well."

"Oh, we do," Brenda said. "But we're realistic about each other. He calls me Tough Broad and I call him Lazy Boy."

Thinking of what Brenda had told her about Tom, Vicky speculated. "Maybe he just didn't find anything that interested him in college."

"Maybe not," Brenda said. "Dad wanted him to be a lawyer. Tom said the only job that ever appealed to him was art critic, but I don't know if he was joking or not. Maybe I'll be the lawyer in the family—if I can get my grades up enough and I don't become a piano teacher instead."

"I don't have a clue about what I want to be," Vicky said.

"How about a tennis pro?" Brenda teased.

"Oh, sure!" Vicky laughed, and they went back to practicing. She missed a shot, thinking of how her mother would react if she told her she was going to make a living at tennis. Dismay, distress, disgust—Mom would *not* approve.

"Hey, are you watching the ball?" Brenda asked when Vicky missed a second time.

"No," Vicky admitted. But on the next ball Brenda sent to her backhand, Vicky came to net and angled her return sharply past Brenda to the outside line.

"Great return," Brenda said. "*Now* do you admit you're improving?"

"Well, I'm not as good a player as you keep saying I am."

"The test'll be how you do in the match on Friday," Brenda said. "Meanwhile, we've both gotta work at keeping that ball low over the net."

"I'm working, I'm working," Vicky assured her taskmaster.

With Brenda the goal was clear and possible to reach. Vicky could enjoy the challenge to improve her tennis. But at the lunch table where she still sat alone with Reggie, the view was murky. Everything seemed normal when they talked about school and impossible homework assignments and weird test questions and teachers' quirks. And sometimes Reggie would still offer an anecdote about Woof's latest exploits—how he'd swiped a leg of lamb when Reggie's mother was on the telephone, or how he'd put long scratches in the kitchen door trying to get out. But whenever the conversation got anywhere near tennis, Reggie's hackles seemed to rise. She would say things like "I don't suppose you want to go for a hike with me this weekend. You'll be too busy with tennis, won't you?" or "Well, you and your jock friends wouldn't be interested in that."

Finally Vicky asked her flat out, "Reggie, does it bother you that I'm getting into tennis so much?"

"I guess," Reggie said.

Out of desperation, Vicky suggested, "Why don't you come and watch us play sometime? Maybe if you understood the game better, I could talk to you about it." The way we used to share everything, Vicky was thinking.

Reggie surprised her by saying, "Okay. When should I come?"

"Well, the team's got a match here on Friday, and I think I'll be playing."

Reggie nodded. "Yeah, I'll do that. First I'll read up on the game, and then I'll watch you play." She looked somewhat relieved, as if she too had hopes of regaining the closeness they'd had.

● ● ● ●

On Friday, when Vicky discovered that her partner in her second team match would be Brenda, her heart leaped into her throat and stuck there. "I can't be your partner," she whispered to Brenda. "What if we lose?"

"Would I ask Sandi for you if I thought we might lose?"

"You *asked* her? But, Brenda, I'm not ready." Vicky's bones went rubbery from fear.

"Yes, you are. All you have to do is return the ball and let them make the errors."

"Maybe in another month—"

"*Now,*" Brenda said. "You're as ready as you'll ever be."

Vicky swallowed and took deep breaths until she regained strength in her limbs. When their opponents—two girls from the middle school in the next town—took warm-up positions near the net, she acknowledged the introductions without hearing their names. But her racket came up automatically. During the five minutes allowed for warm-up before the game started, Brenda kept talking to her cheerfully, even when she missed shots.

When Brenda spun her racket to determine which side would serve first, she and Vicky won. "You be first server, Vicky," Brenda said.

She was where she'd dreamed of being, Vicky told herself, in a tennis match as Brenda's partner. But she served her first two balls into the net.

"Calm down," Brenda whispered to her. "Just think about getting the ball into the right box. Relax and take one shot at a time."

More deep breaths. Why had she ever thought tennis was fun? Vicky asked herself. She'd rather be anywhere but here on this court, making Brenda lose a match.

"You're a good server, Vicky. Serve!" Brenda commanded her.

Vicky served and evened up the score. Fifteen all.

"Get to her backhand. She doesn't have any backhand," Brenda hissed.

Vicky served next toward her opponent's backhand.

"Out," Brenda yelled when the girl's return landed near the baseline. Now they had two points to their opponents' one. "Thirty–fifteen," Brenda called out loud and clear, with a triumphant nod over her shoulder at Vicky.

Brenda put a ball away at net, and by winning the next point, somehow Vicky had won her serve. Shaking a little, she took a sip of water as they changed sides. The water got stuck in her chest.

"We're going to win this. Just play tough," Brenda told her.

One of their opponents sent them a high lob. Vicky thought it touched down on the baseline, but Brenda said the ball was out, and insisted that it was even though the girl who had hit it asked, "Are you sure?"

"Yes, I saw it," Brenda said.

And she was closest to the ball, Vicky told herself. Soon enough they had won five games to their opponents' two. One more game and the set was theirs.

They changed sides and stopped for a drink of water. Vicky's eyes went to a lone figure standing outside the chain-link fence under a tree. Reggie! She had forgotten that Reggie had promised to come and watch this game. "Hey, Reggie," Vicky called, waving.

Reggie nodded. Her arms were folded across her chest and she looked grim.

"That's the girl you eat lunch with, isn't it?" Brenda asked. "The one who's always on the honor roll."

"That's my friend Reggie," Vicky said.

"Does she play tennis?"

"No," Vicky said.

"Are you guys planning to forfeit?" one of their opponents asked impatiently.

"Don't you wish," Brenda said. She grinned at Vicky and said, "Come on. Let's get it together and finish off this set."

To Vicky's amazement, they did easily win the next game, which gave them the first of the two sets they needed to take the match. Vicky looked over at Reggie and gave a thumbs-up sign. Reggie still wasn't looking very happy. Watching wasn't turning out to be much fun for her, apparently.

"Okay," Brenda instructed Vicky on their break between sets. "We've got to finish them off in the second set. I hate going three sets. Besides, these girls aren't that good. Keep hitting to the short one's backhand, Vicky."

The second set was even easier. They won it, 6–0. "See, I *told* you you were ready," Brenda said.

Vicky was thrilled. Brenda's arm across her shoulder felt like a trophy. She looked toward the tree where Reggie had been standing, but Reggie had gone. As soon as she got home, Vicky told herself, she'd call and find out what Reggie had thought of the game. Surely some of it had been exciting to watch.

CHAPTER 7

Friday evening, Vicky was still high from her win. Even Mom noticed. When she happened to glance up from the papers she was marking at the kitchen table, she said, "What's making you look so happy, Vicky? You're positively glowing."

"I won my first tennis match," Vicky said.

"Oh." Mom frowned a little, as if the answer puzzled her. "That's nice, dear," she said, and her eyes drifted back to the stack in front of her.

Vicky sat down at the table opposite her mother and leaned her chin on her crossed forearms. "Mom, do you think they gave you the wrong baby in the hospital?"

Mom's eyes widened behind her glasses. "Vicky! What a thing to ask. You must know how glad I am you're my child."

"But you'd like me better if I were smarter or more talented."

"I like you fine just the way you are," Mom said. She held out her arms, and Vicky went around the table to exchange a hug. It felt good, but somehow Vicky wasn't convinced that her mother would ever have chosen the kind of child who won tennis matches. She'd have picked someone like Reggie if she'd had a choice.

When her mother raised her marking pen once more, Vicky went to call Reggie.

"So what did you think of the game?" Vicky asked.

"It was okay," Reggie said. "Listen, my mother's on call, so she can't drive us to the state park to hike tomorrow. Could your mother do it?"

"How about we just go for a walk along the bike path?" Vicky suggested. She hated adding more chores to her mother's busy weekend.

"Fine. Meet you at the underpass at one?" Reggie said.

"Okay. Now tell me, were you bored? You had a funny look on your face."

The silence at the other end of the wire meant Reggie had something to say that she didn't think Vicky wanted to hear. "We'll talk about it while we're walking," Reggie said.

One of the few habits Reggie had that bothered Vicky was her way of being mysterious and making

Vicky wait to hear the details about something important. But knowing how stubborn Reggie was, Vicky resigned herself to waiting until they met.

● ● ● ●

An overnight frost had killed the grass, leaving it wheat-colored on Saturday morning. But through the mostly leafless trees, the sky was a glassy blue. Vicky enjoyed the run from her house into the suburbs and down River Road a couple of miles to the underpass. She hoped Reggie wasn't going to ruin their time together with whatever she had to say.

As she ran, Vicky was thinking about bringing Reggie and Brenda together so they could get to know each other. After all, two good friends were even better than one. She could enjoy them both, each for her own qualities. Of course, Reggie and Brenda didn't have much in common, except maybe music, but then, she had only a little in common with each of them. With Brenda, it was a passion for tennis. With Reggie, it was a kind of mutual sympathy, a willingness to listen to each other. Or that's how it had been.

It was only fifty degrees out, but Vicky was wearing a T-shirt and shorts. She had a sweatshirt tied around her waist, though, so she wouldn't be too cold when she had to slow down for the walk along the bike path. Her T-shirt was wet with sweat by the time she got to the underpass. Reggie was leaning against the concrete wall waiting for her, dressed in jeans and a sweater over a heavy shirt. Her cheeks had been brightly burnished by the chilly air.

"How long have you been waiting?" Vicky asked her. "You look frozen."

"It's cold standing still here," Reggie said. "My father dropped me off early on his way to work."

It was only a mile from Reggie's house to the underpass. She would have been better off walking it, but Vicky was careful not to say so, because she knew Reggie would take it as a criticism. Instead, she just asked, "So, which way do you want to go?"

"Toward the railroad station, the way we usually go," Reggie said.

They climbed the slope to the bike path and began walking beside the paved trail that had once been a railroad bed. Bike riders blipped by them at regular intervals. They had good views of the river, empty of boat traffic now that summer was over.

Vicky enjoyed watching the gulls wheeling and settling in a flock on the dark, silvery water. She felt too good to rush into whatever negative feelings Reggie had about yesterday's tennis game.

"The math homework was easy," Vicky said. "I did it last night."

"Yeah. I finished it in school." Reggie said. "So are your brother and mother still at it?"

"Still. He keeps giving her a hard time, and she nags him."

"That would drive me nuts."

Vicky was in too good a mood to complain about her family. Cheerfully she said, "Well, it could be worse. Mom could be nagging *me* and Derek could be giving *me* a hard time."

"You mean instead of just ignoring you, as usual?" Reggie asked, as if Vicky were serious.

Vicky winced. Her friend's bluntness had hit a nerve. "I wouldn't say they ignore me. They just sort of . . . take me for granted." She looked at Reggie trudging along beside her with her head down. All that was visible was Reggie's curly hair, the frame of her glasses, and her baggy clothes. "You can't even imagine not being the star of the show, can you?" Vicky asked.

"I guess I am the star—at home, anyway."

"Yeah, you are. You're lucky."

"What about in school? Everybody hates me there. Everybody but you."

"They don't hate you because you're smart. They just—"

"Hate me because they're not," Reggie said. "So, about the game . . ."

"Hmm?" Vicky stalled. She was watching a golden retriever, delirious with joy, bouncing ahead of its master. Vicky wondered when she had ever been half as joyful with Reggie and couldn't think of a single time. Tennis made her joyful, and what else? Nothing came to mind.

"Well, it was fun to see you play," Reggie began. "You looked like you were dancing on the court. I mean, you're really graceful chasing that ball. Even when you miss, you're graceful."

"Thanks." Vicky was pleased by her friend's description.

"But your partner—Brenda."

"She's a very good player," Vicky said quickly.

"Sure. She hits the ball hard and all that, but I saw her call shots out that were really in."

"How would you know what shots were in?"

"I may wear glasses, Vicky, but I can see. A couple of times balls hit the white line and she was looking right at it, and she called them out. The book I read says that if a ball even touches the white line, it's in."

"That can happen to anyone. I mean, a lot

depends on the angle you see it from. You could have been wrong, or Brenda could have made a mistake. It happens."

"She did it twice. Too bad you don't have umpires at tennis matches."

"What are you saying?"

Reggie shrugged. "Look, I know you think she's wonderful, but I'm just telling you what I saw. You don't have to believe me."

"You don't really think Brenda would cheat deliberately, do you?"

"It looked to me like she did."

"She's too good a player, Reggie. And . . . she just wouldn't do that."

Reggie tilted her head doubtfully. "Anyway, it upset me," she said. "Like you won, but . . ."

"But if we cheated to do it, then it wasn't so great."

"*You* didn't cheat. I know *you* wouldn't," Reggie said, and now she met Vicky's eyes. "Listen, maybe I shouldn't have said anything. I know winning's important to you, but I just wanted you to understand why I'm not going to watch any more games."

"Fine with me," Vicky said coolly. She resented Reggie's attitude. She suspected that Reggie was slinging mud at Brenda out of jealousy. At that moment, Vicky didn't like her old friend. She wished their walk was over. Even the homework that waited for her at home would be better than dealing with Reggie's mean suspicions.

• • • •

Saturday evening, Derek said Mom and Vicky should go ahead and eat without him because he was invited to a party and there'd be plenty of food. "It's at this girl's house. You'd like her, Mom. She's an honor student and loaded with manners."

Mom looked at him with glazed eyes over the cardboard box of pizza, which she had just-brought home for the three of them. "Don't leave yet, Derek. I need a few minutes of your time. I have to tell you and Vicky something."

"What?" Derek asked impatiently. "I'm late already. Tomorrow—"

Mom shook her head and swallowed. "Sit down and listen to me. It's not about you this time. It's about me."

That got Derek's attention. He took his usual seat at the kitchen table and fixed his eyes on his mother. Vicky sat down across from her. It struck her that Mom might be sick. Her face had never been so pale, her mouth so drawn, or the line between her eyes so deep.

"My principal had a talk with me yesterday after

school," Mom began in a strained voice. "He wants me to take some personal leave time, a week or two—more if I need it."

"What for?" Derek asked.

"Because some father wrote him a letter, and got other parents to sign it, saying that I'm too strict with their children. He claims his son doesn't want to go to school because of me."

"But you've always been strict," Derek said.

"I've always had an orderly classroom, no matter how many children with difficult behavior problems they assigned to my class."

"Right," Derek said. "So what's different now?"

"The principal. The old one would have taken my part. This man is young, and he listens to the parents. He says my nerves are strained and I need a vacation."

"You could complain to the superintendent. He knows you, Mom," Derek said. His frown resembled his mother's. Vicky was glad that he was responding positively. She herself was too shocked to say a word.

Mom shook her head and closed her eyes. "No. I'm not going to the superintendent. He's not . . . he likes this new principal. I'm going to take personal leave time, as suggested." She opened her eyes, and there were tears in them.

"I came close to striking a child yesterday." She took a shuddering breath. "It could be I'm in the wrong profession for this day and age."

"No, Mom," Derek said with great assurance. "You're a good teacher. You make kids work. They learn a lot in your class. Lots of parents have said that, too. Remember?"

A smile touched her lips. "Thank you for the vote of confidence," she said.

At that, Derek did something he hadn't done in years. He got up and hugged his mother.

"Hey," he said. "It's not so bad. Maybe what you need is to get out of here and go someplace warm. You could visit your cousin in Florida, the one who's always inviting you."

"And what would you and Vicky do?"

"I'll see she doesn't get in any trouble. I'm a big boy, Mom. I can take care of myself and my little sister."

"Derek—"

"No, really. Give me a chance to show I'm not the bum you think I've become. Really. It'd be good for both of us. You *and* me."

"We'll see," Mom said, which was what she usually said when she had decided against something. "You said you were late for your party. Shouldn't you go?"

"Not if you need me here," he said. And suddenly he was sounding like the dependable Derek of Vicky's childhood.

Mom insisted he go to his party, and finally he left.

"It's embarrassing," Mom said to Vicky as she dished out the pizza after heating it in the oven, "to have to tell my children something like this."

"Derek and I still think you're great, Mom."

"You do, Vicky? You think I'm a good mother?"

"You're a good everything," Vicky said. And now that she had a chance, she added, "but you probably ought to lay off Derek."

"Vicky, you don't understand. Your brother's older than you are, so you don't realize what a child he still is."

"He's not a child anymore, and he gets mad when you treat him like one, Mom."

Her mother narrowed her eyes at Vicky. "So I'm failing with my son as well as with my students, according to you?"

"No, that's not what I meant!" Vicky cried.

But it was too late. Her mother spoke from some hollow space inside herself. "The other night you implied that I don't appreciate you," Mom said. "If I'm not good with my own children and not a good teacher, what have I done with my life?" She raised her palm to her cheek and stared wildly at nothing.

In desperation Vicky flung herself at her mother and embraced her, but Mom was limp in her arms, and she pushed Vicky away. "I'm going up to bed now," Mom said. "I'm tired." She patted Vicky's shoulder. "It's all right. I'm just very, very tired." Without thinking, she turned out the lights as she left the kitchen.

Vicky sat in the darkened room. The full moon gave her enough light to see by. If Derek were still here, he'd go to Mom, she thought. He'd know what to say to comfort her. Vicky ached to see her mother so defeated. If only she had the power to ease Mom's pain! But she felt helpless, useless, as if even her love for her mother had no worth.

CHAPTER 8

Monday the tennis courts were wet from the morning's rain. The team had a match across the river after school, but Vicky wasn't scheduled to play. She had other plans, anyway. To her surprise, after their prickly conversation on the bike path, Reggie had called her on Sunday and asked her to go shopping at the mall with her and her father Monday afternoon. Vicky had agreed happily, anxious to set aside whatever bad feelings there were between them.

In the middle of the morning, though, Brenda stopped Vicky in the hall as they were changing classes. "Why don't you come along to watch the match this afternoon? There's room for all of us in the school van."

Vicky explained that she was going to the mall with Reggie.

Brenda looked disgusted. "Hey, where's your

team spirit? Just because you're not playing doesn't mean you don't have to be there."

"Next time I'll come," Vicky said.

But at two o'clock Sandi found her at her locker. "Kelly's got some kind of virus. She's throwing up all over the place. Could you jump in and play for her today? Otherwise we'll have to forfeit a court."

"I don't have my racket," Vicky said.

"You can use hers. It's a Wilson Hammer. That's what you play with, right?"

Vicky hesitated. "Well, I promised a friend . . ."

"Vicky, we'll have to *forfeit a court* if you don't play, which means they start out ahead of us," Brenda said. She had appeared behind Sandi. Two pairs of eyes pleaded with Vicky.

She looked at her gym sneakers right there in her locker along with shorts. "Okay," she said. "Okay."

Hastily she tracked down Reggie and explained why she had to break their date at the last minute. Reggie said she understood. But then she added, "Tennis sure is taking over your life."

"Well, I'm on a team now, so I have to think about other people, Reggie."

"Right," Reggie said. "You're on a team now,

and I guess that's what you always wanted." The tilt she put on that phrase made it sound critical, but Vicky didn't see how she could *not* fill in for a sick player. The team needed her, and she'd agreed to be part of it. Surely that had to take precedence over a trip to the mall. She and Reggie could see each other any time. After all, she didn't play tennis every waking hour of the day.

• • • •

The school van was rumbling over the steel bridge toward the rural area of woods and fields where the middle school they were to compete against was located.

"You might as well be Brenda's partner again," Sandi said over her shoulder to Vicky, who was sitting behind her.

"This is a tough team," Brenda said warily, as if she didn't like Sandi's arrangement.

"Well, who would you put her with, then?" Sandi asked.

Brenda hesitated, frowned, and said, "I guess we'll do okay together."

Vicky squirmed in her seat. It shook her that Brenda didn't want to go into competition with her. What had last Friday been about? Unless Brenda hadn't thought much of her playing. But they'd won! Maybe Brenda thought she'd done all the winning by herself.

Vicky's spirits sank even lower when Sandi collected the team outside the van and told them, "This is going to be our toughest match. Their team came out on top last year. But we can beat them. Just stay cool and remember to keep your feet moving."

So that was it. Brenda had been willing to risk taking Vicky on as a partner for last week's match because it had been an easy one. Now she was probably wishing she hadn't been so generous. Just play your best, Vicky told herself. That's all you can do. But she stepped onto court three feeling inadequate even before she'd seen the pair they were playing against.

The first serve Vicky took came in so hard and low that she hit her return into the net. She took an overhead, but just managed to pop it back, and the girl at the net put it away with ease. Brenda whipped a forehand down the alley, not expecting it to be returned. When it was, she was so surprised that she missed and dropped her racket. Vicky began hanging back, afraid to go to net against these aggressive players. Before she realized it, she and Brenda had lost the first three games.

"What's the matter with you?" Brenda asked her

as they changed from one side of the court to the other. "Just play your game. Move. You can get to any ball they put on the court."

But Vicky couldn't, not that day. She rushed back for an overhead, got to it, but hit it into the net. She charged to get a backhand slice and hit a soft return right to the net person, who slapped it easily down the middle, where both she and Brenda missed it.

"Calm down," Brenda told her. "Don't let them scare you. Just play the ball one point at a time."

Brenda began playing as if she were angry. She smashed a ball at their opponents' feet and won a point. She jumped to take an overhead in the air and angled it across the court for another point. She was fierce and powerful, but they still lost. The game score was now four–love, four for the opponents and none for Vicky and Brenda.

"Take deep breaths and forget the first set. We're going to take this one," Brenda said when she and Vicky had gone down, six–love, in what seemed to Vicky like an instant.

"I can't," Vicky said. "They're too good for me."

"Not if you'd stop blowing every point, they wouldn't be," Brenda snapped. "Come on. We can't lose it this badly. You've got to get tough."

Vicky tried. For Brenda's sake, she tried. She

focused on the ball, telling herself like a mantra, Keep it low. Keep it low. She went to net and didn't let it bother her when she missed and hit it out. She served, but the serve that last week's team couldn't return seemed easy for these girls to get.

"Hit the ball as if you mean it, Vicky," Brenda told her.

"I'm hitting as hard as I can."

"You're playing patty-cake." Brenda was red-faced and grim. She whammed a ball back over the net and out. She angled cross-court and their opponent returned it down the line, and Vicky didn't get to it in time.

"Out," Brenda said with authority, although it looked to Vicky as if the ball had touched the line. Should she have contradicted her partner's call? She wondered, remembering Reggie's suspicions. It didn't matter; they were losing anyway.

The points slipped away as if they were greased and Vicky couldn't get hold of one. She and Brenda lost the second set, 2–6.

"They blew us away," Brenda moaned as if it were a tragedy. "We just let them walk all over us."

"I'm sorry," Vicky said.

"Sorry?" Brenda glared at her. "Being sorry's useless. You've got to be tough if you want to win, Vicky—that is, if you really *do* want to win."

Suddenly Vicky doubted that she did, at least not the way Brenda did. "I know it's my fault we lost," she said, repeating lamely, "I'm really sorry, Brenda. I mean, you deserved a better partner."

Brenda sniffed and seemed to calm down. "You've got to learn to control your nerves in a game, that's all," she said.

They would not be partners again soon, Vicky suspected. Now she had no doubt that the last match had been a setup to give her an easy win against a weak team so she'd gain confidence. All it took was a tough team and she fell apart instantly. She went home depressed. Her life was disintegrating in every direction. She wasn't worthy of being Brenda's partner. Reggie was disgusted with her. And her mother, her strong, dependable mother, seemed to be falling apart.

● ● ● ●

Mom was stretched out on the couch reading when Vicky got home. "Are you okay?" Vicky asked.

"Fine," Mom said as cheerfully as if reading on the couch were her normal day's activity. "And how are you?"

"Okay," Vicky said carefully. She didn't think her mother was in a condition to commiserate with her about losing a tennis game. Mom's eyes returned to her book.

Vicky went to the kitchen and called Reggie to apologize again for not going to the mall and to tell her how awful the tennis match had been. Nobody answered. Vicky left a message on the answering machine and ended by saying, "Call me, Reggie. Please."

But Reggie didn't call.

Derek didn't come home for supper. Vicky fretted about not knowing where he was, but Mom didn't seem to notice his absence. She ate the salad Vicky had cobbled together from leftovers and thanked Vicky and went back to her book and the couch.

Later that night, when she heard Derek's footsteps on the stairs, Vicky got out of bed and stood in the doorway of her room to say, "Mom needs you, Derek."

"There's nothing I can do for her."

"But—"

"Look," he said. "Everybody's got to climb out of their own holes. Leave her alone. She'll be okay."

"She will?"

"Sure," he said, with the old reassuring big brother smile.

• • • •

The next day in class Reggie said, "It's too bad about your tennis match."

"It was a disaster. So what did you get at the mall?"

"Nothing. I didn't see anything I liked."

There were no further invitations from Reggie that week, and the only phone calls were the ones Vicky made to her.

Every afternoon when Vicky got home from school, she found her mother curled up on the couch with a novel. When Vicky asked her how her day had been, she would say sadly, "Okay, I guess. I'm getting caught up on my reading."

"Are you feeling better?" Vicky asked once.

"I wasn't sick, Vicky."

"No, of course not. I didn't mean you were. I just meant . . ." Vicky shrugged and let it go, afraid of making things worse if she continued.

Derek did spend more time at home that week. He regaled Mom and Vicky at dinner with stories about his friends, how this one had put a dent in his mother's brand-new van and that one had gotten a death's-head tattoo. He had broken up with his girlfriend, Derek said. "She wanted me to promise not to see anybody else. I told her I wasn't about to be committed to anything at this stage of my life."

Mom opened her mouth to say something and then closed it. Her eyes went to Vicky, and she chewed on her lip. "Your sister says you're not a boy anymore, Derek," she said. "I hope she's right."

"What do you mean by that, Mom?"

"An adult is committed to being responsible for himself and his family."

Derek looked at Vicky. "You think I'm grown up?" he asked.

"Sometimes you are," she said.

He smiled at her as if her answer pleased him.

In school on Friday, Vicky asked Brenda whether she was still invited for dinner on Sunday.

"Sure you are. Why wouldn't you be?" Brenda said.

"I thought you were mad at me." They'd barely spoken to each other since the match, although they had practiced together on the tennis court before school every morning.

"For what? You mean for losing Monday? I didn't expect we'd win. But the thing is, Vicky, attitude is a big part of it. You've got to want to win, and you don't act like you expect to."

"I guess I don't."

"Well, if you're going to be my partner, you'd better *start* expecting. I hate losing."

Vicky tried to laugh. "No kidding!"

Brenda just looked at her. She wasn't amused.

Vicky took a deep breath. "I'm not the right partner for you, Brenda."

"We'll see," Brenda said airily.

• • • •

Brenda's brother, Tom, opened the door for Vicky on Sunday evening. He gave her a smile as wide as his face. "I hope you're ready for this," he said. "It's a clam pizza."

Vicky asked bravely, "With garlic?"

"Lots of garlic."

"Good," she said. "I like garlic." She hoped she wouldn't throw up before she got home. Clams were one of the few things that disagreed with her.

"The folks are having a cocktail in the living room," Tom said. "Can I get you a soda or something?"

"No, thank you." She followed him into the high-ceilinged living room, which was elegantly decorated in muted blues and grays. Tom introduced her to his mother, a large, handsome woman with a genial smile and a welcoming twinkle in her blue eyes. His father put down his newspaper and reached across his long legs to shake Vicky's hand.

"Any friend of Brenda's is a friend of the family," he said in a deep, hearty voice.

They quizzed her casually by way of making conversation.

She told them that her mother was a teacher and she had never known her father. It had always been awkward for her when people asked about her father. Sometimes the reaction was shock and sometimes pity. This time she saw both in their eyes and added, "I'm lucky. My mother's enough for me."

"I'm sure she is," Brenda's mother said encouragingly.

Tom put a plate of canapés in front of Vicky. "These are just cheese puffs," he said. "Pretty simple."

"Tom's always been interested in cooking," his mother said. "We thought he might become a chef, but—"

"Eating's more my thing." Tom said. "The pizza will be out of the oven in ten minutes." He left the room.

"So you're Brenda's tennis partner. Where did you learn to play?" Brenda's father asked.

"At school, a few years ago, when Brenda did."

"Then why haven't we seen you before?" Brenda's father asked.

"Well, I had some problems, so I was out of the game for part of last year."

"How nice that you're back in it," Brenda's mother said.

Vicky was glad when Tom called them to the dining room. He had a big salad to go with the pizza, which tasted so delicious that she forgot her wariness about eating clams. "This is outrageous," she said. "I never knew pizza could taste so good."

"It's nice to have company," Tom said. "I never get compliments like that from the home folk."

Afterward, when Brenda was walking Vicky home, Vicky said, "I wish I had a brother like Tom."

Brenda laughed. "No, you don't. My parents are ready to kill him. All they talk about is how to get him to go to work. I could tell them I won Wimbledon and they'd nod and keep talking about Tom."

"But he's nice to you."

"Isn't your brother nice to you?"

"Sometimes. He used to be *all* the time. I don't

know. Maybe he just got sick of having me hanging around looking up to him."

"Yeah, that's got to be a drag, having to live so you'll be looked up to. It should only happen to me."

"I look up to you," Vicky said shyly. "I think you're a great tennis player."

"Well, thanks," Brenda said. "Listen, don't sweat it, Vicky. Your big brother will truck off to college in a couple of years, whereas mine's likely to muck up our family life forever."

"But why? Just because he doesn't have a job?"

"Yeah, and because he doesn't have any friends or any ambition or any goals. And because he weighs three hundred pounds and won't go for therapy."

"I guess he must be unhappy about something."

"Isn't everybody?"

"What are you unhappy about?" Vicky asked.

"Well, I'm no special beauty and no great brain, and I need to be tops at something."

"Tennis?" Vicky asked.

"Who knows? I play the piano pretty well. I've got an okay singing voice. But what I like best is hitting a tennis ball."

"You're lucky to be good at more than one thing."

"I need to be *best* at one thing," Brenda said. "Don't you?"

"Yes," Vicky said, realizing that somewhere inside her, that was what she did want. "Yes," she said with more conviction. And she felt glad that she and Brenda had that in common.

● ● ● ●

Before she took a shower that night, Vicky called Reggie to ask how she was doing. "Fine," Reggie said shortly.

"You're mad at me, aren't you?"

"Sort of."

"Well, I'm sorry, Reggie."

"Hmm." Reggie sighed. "Look, I can't help being jealous. You've gotten tied up with other people. I don't blame you. Only I wish you'd left room in your life for me."

"Reggie, I do have room for you."

"I don't think so—not really. See you in school, Vicky." And Reggie hung up.

What had she done? Vicky asked herself. Reggie and she had had such an easygoing relationship. There was no pressure when she spoke to Reggie, just the ebb and flow of school concerns and whether to get a shorter haircut or see a movie someone had recommended.

It was an easier friendship than she could possibly have with Brenda. Brenda set up hoops that she expected Vicky to jump through. And winning was so important to her.

Well, really, what was so bad about winning? Vicky asked herself. She'd liked the one taste she'd had so far well enough. But if it meant losing friends? That was a question she wasn't ready to answer yet.

CHAPTER 9

Sandi had asked the team to attend a lunchtime meeting to plan strategy for the following Friday's match with Shenendehowa. She said it was important to beat that team, which had also won two matches and lost two, because then their team would remain in the top half of team rankings. The loser would slip into the bottom half.

"How about eating at Sandi's table with me today?" Vicky said to Reggie. "I've got to be there for a team meeting."

"So go," Reggie said. "I'll eat at our regular table."

"Alone?"

Reggie sighed. "Do you think I'm a total outcast, Vicky? You're not the only person in the whole school willing to talk to me."

"Well, of course not, but—"

"Don't worry about it. Go to your meeting," Reggie said.

Vicky went, feeling vaguely guilty. Over her shoulder she saw Reggie sitting down at the table near the door—alone.

"So what do you think?" Sandi asked the eight team members who were eating lunch at the table. "We'll probably win one of the two singles match-es. Should we put our best players on second- and third-court doubles and figure on losing first and taking the other two?"

"You're the captain," Sonja said.

"I'd like to play first-court doubles," Brenda said. "With Vicky."

Everyone looked at her. "I was planning on you and me on second," Sandi said. "That's if we go with this strategy."

"You can win second court with Kelly or Bette. Vicky and I are going to win on first."

"I don't think so," Vicky said. She was so over-come by the fear of losing that she added, "I think I should sit this one out."

"She's played two in a row," Sandi said to Brenda. "I wasn't planning to play Vicky in this one."

"It's like getting back on a horse that threw you," Brenda said. "You have to do it right away or you don't get over being scared."

Sandi chewed her thumbnail, thinking. "All

right," she said. "We'll do it your way, Brenda. I'll play second court with Kelly. Mari and Jo can take third, and you and Vicky can try your luck on first. The singles players keep on as usual."

"Vicky and I are going to win," Brenda said.

"I hope so," Sandi said. She smiled at Vicky. "Anyway, you've got four days to rev yourself up for it."

"Maybe it'll rain," Vicky said fervently. Everybody laughed except Brenda.

"It's not going to rain," she said. "Start thinking positively."

Vicky groaned. "Okay," she said. "Okay. It will rain. It will rain. It will rain."

"Yay, team!" Bette said, and laughed.

"Are we playing at home, or do we have to go to Shenendehowa?" Kelly asked.

"We're home. Let's everyone show up for practice this week. Okay?" Sandi said.

● ● ● ●

"Why did you ask for court one?" Vicky asked Brenda as they pushed their way through the crowded hall toward the girls' room.

"Because. I was reading this article about how tennis is all a head game, and they could have been talking about you. You're so sure you're not good enough that you set yourself up to lose. I figure we've got four days to change your mind."

"Four days isn't enough," Vicky muttered. "You'll hate me if we lose."

"I'll hate you more if you don't try."

"But, Brenda, you could win with someone else."

Brenda's confident smile transformed her broad face into something beautiful. She looked like her handsome mother when she smiled. "I want to win with *you*," she said.

Vicky got tears in her eyes. "Thanks," she said. She felt as if Brenda had just announced that they had become friends—not just tennis buddies, but real friends. And Vicky was grateful. Now, if only she could live up to Brenda's belief in her.

At the next practice, Brenda kept instructing Vicky to get to the net faster and angle the ball instead of hitting it straight back to the player on the other side. "Keep moving, Vicky," she urged. Brenda didn't move fast herself, but she hit hard enough to put a ball away whenever she got near one. Meanwhile, Vicky had to cover three quarters of the court and keep the ball in play. But with Vicky whizzing around and Brenda whacking balls with grim determination, they were winning.

"You're doing great together," Sandi told them in some surprise. And when practice was over, several other team members complimented them.

"See, I told you," Brenda said to Vicky. "It's simple. You set me up and I make the point."

Vicky nodded. She felt good. "We're going to win, win, win," she murmured.

"Just keep saying it," Brenda said. "And remind yourself what a good player you are."

"Well, I'm steady and I get to the balls," Vicky said. She was confident that Brenda would do the rest.

● ● ● ●

On Wednesday before school they practiced serve and volley. Thursday before school was team practice. They beat Sandi and Kelly, 6–4, and Vicky went home feeling powerful. The next morning she and Brenda would practice their cross-courts, and on Friday afternoon they would win on first court against a fairly tough team.

"You look like an overtightened guitar string about to snap," Derek said to Vicky Thursday evening as they were doing the dishes together.

Mom was still in retirement on the couch. "What's up with you?" he asked.

"I have a tennis match I need to win tomorrow."

"So what's the big deal if you don't? You're not planning to turn pro, are you?"

"No. I just need to win this match."

"How come?"

"To prove something to myself, Derek."

"That you've got some guts?"

"Something like that."

"Well," he said. "I hope you do win."

She looked at him to see if he was mocking her. He didn't seem to be. "Thanks," she said cautiously.

"Don't mention it."

"Do you think this staying home from work is helping Mom?" Vicky asked him.

"I doubt it. I think she's burned out as a teacher. Maybe it'd be different if she had a principal who appreciated her. I mean, Mom's good at a lot of stuff. She really gets work out of kids, and she keeps them in line." He looked toward the living room, where he'd spent time each evening that week talking to their mother.

"I'm glad you're being nicer to her, Derek."

"Why? Was I being mean?"

"I thought you were."

He shrugged. "I just can't take being nagged all the time. You're lucky, Vicky. She's never after you."

"Because she doesn't think she can make much out of me. You're the one she expects to do her proud."

He looked at her strangely through narrowed eyes. "Could be she's banking on the wrong kid," he said. And again he didn't seem to be mocking her.

CHAPTER 10

Brenda and Vicky arrived first, as usual, for their match after school on Friday. Brenda had on the team's colors, red and white—red tennis skirt and white top. Vicky had done her best with white shorts and a red T-shirt.

"You look happy, Brenda," Vicky said.

"I *am* happy. How do you feel?"

"Nervous." Vicky felt shaky and sick to her stomach.

"Take ten deep breaths."

"Oh, Brenda."

"Come on. I read it in an article. Let's go. I'll do them with you."

On the tenth breath Vicky agreed that she did feel better.

"Okay, now, remember, whatever happens, keep chasing that ball. Don't get defensive. Don't get cautious, just hit hard and keep moving."

"What if they're better than we are?"

"They can't be. We're the best."

"I'm not, Brenda."

"Oh, yes, you are." Brenda said it with such assurance that Vicky wondered if it could be true. Could she have improved that much?

"Anyway, I'm going to try," Vicky said.

"You mean you're going to *win*. Right?"

"Right," Vicky said, and they slapped high fives. Their opponents on court one arrived wearing black-and-white-checked shirts and black skirts. They looked sharp, and in warm-up they didn't miss a single ball. Brenda pointed at the tall African American girl with cornrows in her hair. "Keep the ball away from her if you can. She's good."

Immediately Vicky's nerves went off like fireworks. It was hard to keep in mind that she was going to win.

The afternoon couldn't have been more perfect for a tennis match. The air seemed to gleam, and the blue sky above them was as clear as glass. With the beeches and maples shedding the last of their crimson, gold, and mahogany leaves, the world was rich in color. Vicky vibrated with excitement. She almost believed they might win the match as she waited in the forehand court for the first serve. It came hard, right at her. She returned it, but barely. The net person, a short girl with a permanent frown, took a step to the middle and sent the ball down the alley past Brenda for the point. When it was Brenda's turn to receive serve, she hit her return into the net. Vicky managed to get the third serve and tried to lob it, but the girl with the cornrowed hair took two quick steps back and whacked the ball down at her feet. It was forty–love; one more point and the game was lost. Brenda took the next serve— and hit it into the net again.

"We've got to loosen up," she muttered as she and Vicky changed to the other side.

"I'm trying," Vicky said.

"Try harder," Brenda snapped.

It seemed to Vicky that losing the first game had been mostly Brenda's fault, but she smiled and teased, "Try harder, loosen up, and win, win, win. Will do!" But Brenda wasn't smiling back at her.

"You can serve first for our side," Brenda told her.

The short girl on the other team missed Vicky's serve. Brenda came to the baseline to say, "That's the way, Vicky. Now, put it down the middle, and I'll poach."

Vicky's second serve didn't quite go down the middle, but Brenda lunged at the return and got a piece of it. Her hit went in, died, and made another point for their side. She looked back at Vicky and winked.

"Down the middle again," Brenda mouthed silently.

This time Vicky got the ball where Brenda wanted it, but the cornrowed girl slammed it back at Brenda and won the point. No directives from Brenda on where to serve. Vicky tried one to the outside line, and again the short girl missed.

"Keep it up—you're doing good," Brenda said.

Vicky tried one to the cornrowed girl's backhand, but the girl returned it as a high lob. Vicky managed to run down behind Brenda and across court to reach the ball. It had been a spectacular get, but her return was weak enough for an easy putaway by the cornrowed girl, who had materialized at net in anticipation of it. The score was 40–30 in favor of Vicky and Brenda. Vicky directed her serve right at the short girl, who sent it back high to the baseline. Brenda, looking over her shoulder, called, "Out."

The ball hadn't looked out to Vicky. She stared at the line uncertainly, but she didn't argue. The game score was one to one, and Brenda had regained her confidence.

The African American girl had a slice on her serve that neither Vicky nor Brenda could handle.

Brenda got the third serve back, but Vicky hit the next shot into the net. Two games to one. They changed sides.

"Okay," Brenda said. "Try to poach, Vicky. You're fast. You can do it." She served, and the cornrowed girl returned it down the line just as Vicky was moving toward the middle to take the return at net. The next time she tried to poach, the same thing happened.

"Forget poaching," Brenda said tensely. "You'd better stand farther back."

They lost that game and the next. When it was the African American girl's turn to serve, she sliced one that Vicky thought landed on the white line at the corner of the court. "Out," Brenda yelled.

Vicky turned to look at her partner questioningly.

The African American girl challenged Vicky. "How do you call it?"

"I don't know," Vicky said uneasily. But loyalty to Brenda made her add, "My partner says it was out."

The black girl bounced the ball twice, three times, five times, to register her anger at Brenda's call. Vicky suddenly felt sick to her stomach. She wasn't supposed to overrule her partner unless she was sure, and she hadn't been absolutely sure, and yet. . . .

The game score was 4–1 in their opponents' favor. Vicky hit a ball that landed on the outside line—on the white, as she saw it. The short girl said calmly, "Out."

Tit for tat, Vicky thought, and didn't let it bother her. Brenda was chewing her lip. She smashed an overhead well inside the back line for a winning point and evened up the score. "Deuce," the server announced.

Brenda had moved in back of the service line because their opponents had started to lob. "Out," Brenda called as the lob came down— right on the baseline. Vicky was certain of it, but she was at net, and Brenda was standing there looking at where the ball had landed.

The African American girl said, "Okay, that's it. One more like that and I'm getting someone to watch the line calls for us."

"I'm calling them as I see them," Brenda said calmly.

"You must be cockeyed, then," the cornrowed girl snapped.

"Come on, let's play and get this over with," her partner said in disgust.

Embarrassed, Vicky whispered, "Brenda, let's give them the benefit of the doubt from now on."

"No way," Brenda said. "Don't let them psych

you out. I call them as I see them." Defiantly, she added, "And we're going to win this."

Somehow Brenda seemed to thrive on suspicion. She played so well that they took that game. They still had only two games to their opponents' four, but the cornrowed girl began slamming ball after ball out of the court or into the net. Her anger was destroying her game.

Vicky played steadily, although she felt as miserable as she ever had on a tennis court, even when she and Brenda finally took the set, 7–5.

"I told you we could win this," Brenda said with enthusiasm. "See, it's all a head game."

"Be careful that girl doesn't slam the ball down your throat," Vicky said.

Brenda grinned and said, "I'll slam it right back."

They lost the second set, 6–0, so fast that Vicky couldn't recall a single point.

In the third set, Brenda made a line call at the baseline on the backhand side that the cornrowed girl questioned. Again she looked at Vicky, asking, "How did you see that?"

"I didn't," Vicky said, relieved that she hadn't.

"Okay, if that's how it's going to be," the girl replied, and she started calling line shots out that were clearly in.

They were being watched, now that the other

courts had finished their matches. Vicky had no idea whether her team was winning or losing. She felt ashamed of how she and Brenda had won some of their points, and she hit the ball mechanically, trying not to think. The short girl began popping balls up over Brenda's head, but Vicky got to most of them and returned them well. When the short girl didn't manage to get them high enough, Brenda took them as overheads midcourt and slammed them back for wins.

They won the third set in a tiebreaker, 7–6. Brenda was exultant. She raised her arms in the air and shouted for joy. Vicky couldn't meet her opponents' eyes. She glanced at Sandi, but Sandi's face was impassive. The cornrowed girl was expostulating to her captain.

"Sore losers," Brenda said firmly. "How'd the team do?"

"We lost," Sandi said. "We took one singles and your match, and they got the rest."

"Too bad," Brenda said. "Oh, well, there's always the chance their team'll mess up next spring, when it really counts."

"Right," Sandi said.

Brenda put her arm over Vicky's shoulders. "Cheer up," she said. "It was a good match. I told you we could win."

Vicky tried to smile, but she felt bad. Worse, she felt slimy. In the time it had taken to play the game, her admiration for Brenda had curdled into something sour.

• • • •

That night at dinner Derek surprised her by asking how she had done in the match that afternoon.

"Brenda and I won, but our team lost."

"Yeah? You won? Good for you," Derek said. "Maybe I ought to come watch you sometime if you're getting that good."

"Oh, Derek. I'm not that good. And you'd be bored."

"Not if you're good, I wouldn't be." His smile felt to her like a ray of sun after days of rain.

"It's nice that you play tennis," Mom said. Vicky was as surprised by her comment as she had been by Derek's.

"How come, Mom?" Derek asked. "I thought academic achievement was all you cared about."

"It's good to be well balanced," Mom said.

"Are *you* well balanced, Mom?" Derek asked in a teasing way.

Earnestly, Mom answered him. "I've decided I should become more so. I think that may be what's gone wrong. I'm too narrowly focused. As a matter of fact, I plan to start swimming at the Y after school. Did I tell you I'm going back to work on Monday?"

"But you've only been home for two weeks, Mom," Derek said.

"That was enough," Mom said. "I'm tired of reading all day."

"Good for you! I figured you were too tough to stay down and out for long," Derek said. He got up from the table and began to clear the dishes.

Mom thanked him with a smile. Then she turned to Vicky. "And thank you for seeing to the care and feeding of your weary mother," she said.

Vicky was pleased. She hadn't thought her mother had noticed.

● ● ● ●

In homeroom on Monday morning, Reggie leaned across the aisle between their desks and said, "I hear you played a tough match and won last Friday. Congratulations."

"Thanks," Vicky said. "But who told you?" She knew Reggie usually didn't follow school sports events.

"I heard a couple of your teammates on the bus this morning. They seem to think you're really good."

Vicky's eyes filled. Her impulse was to tell Reggie about the worm in her apple, but she stopped herself. Reggie's open, full-cheeked face inclined toward hers inquisitively, as if she sensed that Vicky had something to confide. But all Vicky said was, "Thanks, Reggie."

Reggie's face fell, and she pulled back. Vicky was sorry to disappoint her, but she couldn't admit that she suspected her partner of cheating when Reggie already was sure Brenda did.

At lunch Brenda grabbed Vicky's arm and steered her toward the table where Sandi was sitting with some of their teammates. "Want to come over to my house after school, Vicky?" Brenda asked. "I've got another tennis video we could study."

"No, thanks," Vicky said. She looked around for Reggie, thinking she'd excuse herself and go sit with her, but Reggie was nowhere to be seen.

"Okay, well, if you're busy . . ." Brenda sounded miffed.

"Maybe later in the week," Vicky said, just to be polite.

It was drizzling when she left school. She went home and got her racket and a couple of cans of old balls and took herself to the school's backboard. She needed to work her way out of her black mood, and hitting a tennis ball was the only way she knew to do it. Had Brenda cheated—deliberately or not? Had she herself cheated by not contradicting Brenda's calls?

If she'd said she saw a ball as good that Brenda had called out, the other team would have gotten the point automatically. Then Vicky would have felt okay, but Brenda would have been furious. And would she have been justified? It could be that Brenda had actually seen the balls as out. Sometimes people believed they saw things the way they wanted them to be. Or it could be that Vicky was wrong and the balls *had* been out, just barely. Maybe Brenda had a better eye for judging line calls than she did. Brenda had been so confident. She hadn't acted guilty, the way Vicky would have if she'd made a dishonest call.

But what if Brenda had seen them land on the line and had called them out just because she wanted to win so much? It was a rotten way to win. It blew the joy out of it. Vicky was half inclined to confront Brenda and ask her outright whether she'd cheated or not. But if she hadn't—if Brenda had really called the balls as she'd seen them—then she'd be so insulted. And if Brenda *had* cheated, what would she say? She might lie and say she hadn't. If cheating didn't bother her, then lying wouldn't, either. And if she'd cheated and she admitted it, what then?

Then Vicky would know that she could never play with Brenda again.

She'd been hitting one ball steadily for so long against the backboard that it had gotten soggy in the drizzle. Vicky retired it and took out a second ball. She practiced her cross-courts against the backboard. The rhythm was soothing, and the solution finally floated to the surface of her mind. She wouldn't say anything to Brenda. She'd just ask Sandi to let her try singles when it was her turn to play another match.

"I think I'm basically a singles player," she'd tell Sandi. And if Sandi didn't want her in a singles spot, well, then, she'd drop off the team. The idea made her feel sick to her stomach, but she told herself that next fall in high school she could try out for doubles again if she felt like it. By then Brenda would have found another partner. It was rotten. The whole thing was rotten, and it wasn't fair that winning should be this way. Still, Vicky couldn't see any other way out.

CHAPTER 11

Tuesday night at the dinner table, Mom said, "I think the break was good for me. Yesterday when I walked into class, the students booed—at least a few of them did." She smiled a pained smile, and added, "It hurt me. But today I got this note."

She offered it first to Derek, who was finishing up the stew Mom had made over the weekend. He glanced at the sheet of notebook paper while he was still chewing. "Nice, Mom." He passed the letter to Vicky.

The note read, *Dear Mrs. Baylor, We're sorry about yesterday. We were glad to see you back. We think you're a good teacher. Your students.* There were five signatures below the closing. They were all girls, Vicky noted. "Good, Mom. They *do* appreciate you," she said.

"Some of them, anyway," Mom agreed, and this time her smile was happier.

"So you gonna ease up a little on them?" Derek asked her.

"A little," Mom said. "I can't compromise my standards, but I mean to apply them more gently."

Derek nodded. "Say, I meant to tell you. I tried that CD-ROM you got me. I did okay on the sample tests. So I guess I'll take the SATs next time they're given, after the first of the year."

"Yes, Derek!" Mom sounded relieved. "Yes. Then if you don't do well, you'll have time to—"

"Mom," he cut off any unnecessary advice, "I'm going to do well."

"Of course," she agreed immediately. "I know you will, Derek."

Their civility soothed Vicky's frayed nerves. This was more like it, the way she wanted her family to sound. As for her own problem, she didn't think either her mother or her brother would understand why she felt as if a gift she'd been given had blown up in her hands. Besides, she had already decided what to do. Discussing it would only be painful.

● ● ● ●

On Wednesday morning, Sandi rushed up to Vicky in the hall. "Can you show up for team practice after school today, Vicky? You won't believe this, but Mr. Finn is finally granting us some of his precious time. I told him we only have one more match before the season is over, but he says he's thinking ahead to the spring."

Mr. Finn was such a cranky sort of man that his neglect hadn't bothered anybody on the team. "The less we see of him, the better" was how Bette had once put it. The soccer and cross-country teams, whom he had been coaching all fall, were always complaining about him. They said he was fussy and turned what should have been fun into boring lectures and tedious exercises.

"I can be there," Vicky said, "but, Sandi, I wanted to talk to you about something."

"What?"

"Would it be okay for me to try singles for a change?"

"Why? You and Brenda are doing fine together, aren't you?"

"I guess, but . . ." Vicky stumbled and stopped. Then she said, "I just think I'd do better at singles."

"Maybe you would. . . . Okay." Sandi looked at her uncertainly. "Does Brenda know?"

"No, I thought you could just say how the line-up would be next spring."

"She won't go for that," Sandi said. "You'd

better talk to her first, Vicky. She's the one who told me that you make good partners."

"Well, we do. I mean, Brenda's strong. She knows how to put a ball away, and I'm steady, but . . ."

Sandi shook her head. "You've got to talk to her yourself," she repeated.

Vicky sighed and agreed that she would, even though it was what she had been trying to avoid.

At practice on Wednesday afternoon, Mr. Finn arrived wearing a bulky warm-up suit, gloves, and a cap with earflaps.

"Do you believe this guy?" Brenda whispered to Vicky.

"I guess because he's so thin, he gets cold easily," Vicky said. It was not quite fifty degrees out, and windy to boot. She was wearing her warm-up suit over a sweater and was sorry she hadn't brought gloves herself.

"Okay, girls. I've come to check you out, see how you're doing. Go ahead and play with your regular partners and I'll observe," Mr. Finn said.

"Can we warm up first?" Sandi asked.

"Absolutely. You've always got to warm up. In fact . . ." He then proceeded to put them through stretching exercises, which used up ten minutes of the precious hour they had before the late buses left. There were mutterings in the ranks, but he was in charge, so they stretched their hamstrings and jogged in place as he directed. Fifteen more minutes went in warm-up at the net before Mr. Finn let them play any games.

"Okay, Vicky, let's show our stuff," Brenda said. "You start serving."

Sandi hadn't said anything about her playing singles, and it seemed like an awkward time to announce that she wanted to try it, so Vicky obediently served up the first ball. They were playing opposite Sandi and Kelly.

"What's the matter with you today?" Brenda asked with concern when they had lost the first two games, mainly because Vicky was hitting out or into the net. "You nervous because Finn is watching?"

"I guess," she said.

"Lucky for us it's not a match." Brenda smiled. "Relax, we don't have to impress *him.*"

Brenda was playing at the top of her form. She even ran to get a lob, and her backhand crosscourt was lethal. Sandi and Kelly started directing most of their balls to Vicky, who either returned them weakly or missed them. She couldn't remember when she'd played this badly. She forgot about not wanting to be Brenda's partner and started trying to keep her eye on the ball, follow through, bend her knees, keep the ball low over the net—all those basics she and Brenda had been working so hard to integrate into their game.

Mr. Finn called them together to hear his critique just five minutes before the late buses were due to leave. "What you need," he told them in his high-pitched voice, "is to learn to move as if you're yoked together."

Now, Vicky told herself. *Speak up now and get it over with.*

"Your partner moves to the left to take a ball and you move to the left with her," Mr. Finn continued while the girls looked restlessly toward the line of yellow buses. "She goes back to take an overhead, you back up, but be ready to go forward—always forward to the net. That's the strong position. Tomorrow morning we'll go through some drills so that you can get the feel of moving as if you're yoked together."

"Mr. Finn," Vicky said desperately. "I'd like to try singles, if that's okay."

"What?" Brenda exclaimed. "Oh, come on, Vicky. Don't get discouraged just because you were off one day. We're good together."

"No, really," Vicky said. "I think I'd do better as a singles player. Doubles just isn't my thing."

Brenda's face stiffened. She didn't say anything else, but she was obviously hurt.

"We can try you out in singles tomorrow, Vicky," Sandi said cheerfully. She eyed Brenda. "It's just as well to get practice with more than one partner, Brenda. You pick someone else you want to play with."

"It makes no difference to me," Brenda said coldly. She turned away and walked toward the buses. As if she'd given them a signal, the other girls ran for the buses without waiting for Mr. Finn to get around to dismissing them.

Sandi looked at Vicky and asked, "You're sure this is worth it?"

"I don't know," Vicky said. Her eyes stung with unshed tears, and her stomach churned.

"Listen, what's going on here?" Mr. Finn asked. "So what if you didn't play well today, Vicky? That's no big deal. Everybody has an off day now and then."

"I know," Vicky said. "Please excuse me. I've got to go." She dashed away from the courts, picking up her belongings as she ran. She knew that if she heard another word from either Sandi or Mr. Finn, she'd start bawling.

● ● ● ●

Mom was out food shopping that evening. When the phone rang, Derek answered it. "It's for you," he said to Vicky with a hop of his eyebrows to mock her. "A guy. A deep-voiced guy."

"I don't know any guys," she said, taking the receiver.

"Vicky? This is Tom, Brenda's brother, the clam pizza cook?"

"Oh. Hi, Tom," she said, wondering why he was calling. "How are you?"

"I'm fine. But Brenda's in a funk. She says you're mad at her about something, and she doesn't know what, and you don't want to be her tennis partner anymore."

Vicky swallowed. What could she say? She couldn't tell Tom she thought his sister cheated. She squirmed and swallowed and said, "It's no big deal. I thought I'd try playing singles for a change. That's all."

"Yeah, well, I don't know anything about tennis, but . . ." His voice coaxed gently. "Maybe if you came over and told her you still like her or something?"

"Right now?"

"I'll come and get you in the car and drive you home when you're ready to leave," he said quickly.

Vicky barely had time to think about what she could say to Brenda before Tom was ringing the doorbell. She introduced him to Derek, who looked him up and down critically. Derek kept in shape by running, and he rarely ate desserts. Vicky knew he was thinking that Tom was obese.

"Tom's a wonderful cook," Vicky said in his defense.

Tom smiled. "Your sister's a diplomat," he said. "I need her to oil the troubled waters in my house. When my sister gets into a black mood, we all suffer.

"So what's going on between you and Brenda?" Tom asked Vicky in the car.

She took a deep breath. She could evade his question, but on impulse she decided not to. "Brenda and I feel differently about how you play a game. I think winning's a lot more important to her than it is to me." That was putting it as close to the truth as she dared go.

"She put too much pressure on you?"

"Something like that."

"Brenda's got some great qualities," he said thoughtfully. "She'd turn the world upside down for someone she cares about, but she does get intense about whatever she does. Tennis, music, having a friend. . . . She really likes you a lot, Vicky."

"I like *her* a lot," Vicky said. "Except—"

"Except you don't want to be her tennis partner."

"Hmm," Vicky said.

"Well, maybe you can talk to her about it and make her feel better. Anyway, give it a try, okay?"

"Okay," Vicky said.

When they got to the house, Vicky marched up the curved staircase and knocked on Brenda's bedroom door. "Who is it?" Brenda asked. The momentous sounds of a Beethoven symphony went silent.

"It's me. Vicky."

The door opened. Brenda's eyes were red, and she looked upset. Vicky was moved. She had never seen Brenda being miserable. She had imagined that she was invulnerable.

"How come you're here?" Brenda asked.

"Your brother's worried about you."

"Oh, Tom!" Brenda snorted. "He's such a mother hen. I'm fine. I mean, it's no big deal if you don't want to be my partner anymore."

"Brenda," Vicky said, "I like you a lot, and I was glad to be your partner. But . . ."

"But what?" She opened the door wider and Vicky followed her into the bedroom. Brenda perched on the corner of her bed and focused her whole attention on Vicky, who sat down as if she were taking the witness chair.

"In that match," Vicky began breathlessly, because it seemed that she had no choice but to come out with it. "I thought your line calls weren't—I felt as if you were calling things out just to give us some points." There, she'd said it. It didn't sound so terrible laid out like that.

"You think I'm a cheat."

Put that way, it did sound terrible.

Vicky took a deep breath. "Did you *really* see those balls as out?"

"Yes, or I wouldn't have called them that way." Brenda stared her straight in the eye, unsmiling.

Vicky took a deep breath. "Good," she said. "I'm glad you didn't cheat deliberately. I didn't expect you would."

"Okay," Brenda said. "So now do you think I'm a liar as well as a cheat?"

"Oh, no. Of course not, Brenda." Vicky felt compelled to reassure them both because to still be doubtful was shameful.

Brenda shrugged. "Well, are you still set on playing singles?"

It was a tough question. Vicky hesitated. "Well, how about you? Do you want me as a partner now?"

Brenda jutted her lower lip out. "If you keep

playing the way you did in practice today? No."

Vicky laughed and let go of her suspicions. "Okay," she said lightly. "I'll try to do better."

"A lot better," Brenda insisted. She grinned, and Vicky grinned back at her. Somehow they had made it past the danger point and were friends again. Vicky went home with Tom, feeling lighthearted.

"You guys fixed it?" Tom asked in the car.

"Yeah, I think we fixed it," she said.

"Good. I was getting pretty sick of Beethoven. Maybe she'll switch to Mozart for a change."

Vicky laughed. Brenda was lucky to have him for a brother, even if he hadn't found a job that suited him yet.

● ● ● ●

The next morning Vicky told Sandi that she and Brenda were still a pair, at least for a while longer.

"Was it about her line calls?" Sandi asked Vicky.

Vicky was surprised by Sandi's question. She didn't know how to answer.

"I've played with Brenda," Sandi said enigmatically. "If you decide you want to play singles, you can." Sandi smiled. "Anyway, you'll find out soon enough. I'd like you and Brenda to play our last match this Friday. We're short two girls. Would you believe hairdressers' appointments?"

It wasn't promising, Vicky thought. Brenda had said that she didn't cheat, but Sandi had implied that she did. Vicky felt as if she were in a maze. She wondered how she would ever work her way out of it, and if she would have any friends left if she did.

CHAPTER 12

Vicky opened her eyes on Thursday morning, chilled into wakefulness by the thought that she was losing Reggie's friendship. It was unraveling as fast as the cut end of a knitted sweater. Not only had Reggie stopped calling her, but when Vicky made the phone calls, Reggie was only polite and very distant.

Few girls were as lovable and understanding as Reggie. She'd been the one Vicky had talked to when she couldn't confide in her mother or brother. There had to be some way to repair a friendship like theirs, which held years of shared experiences. It would be stupid to lose it just because Vicky was afraid to tell Reggie something that might make her angry. If Vicky could level with Brenda, who was a new friend, then surely she could tell her dear old friend how she felt.

Instead of going to school at seven to hit some

tennis balls, Vicky called Reggie and announced, "We've got to talk."

"About what?"

"About us."

"Huh?"

"Reggie, this is important. Please, could you get to school early today?"

"I guess," Reggie said grudgingly.

They met on the broad front steps of the school. Reggie was wearing her heavy wool sailor jacket in the early morning chill. Vicky had on an old windbreaker of her brother's over a skirt and sweater.

"Let's walk," Vicky said.

Reggie frowned at her anxiously. "So what do you want to talk about?"

"Come on." Vicky led her away from the front steps of the school, where people could hear what they were saying, around the corner, and down the avenue of trees. There they had only early morning dog-walkers to contend with.

"I want to tell you that you're not being fair and it makes me angry," Vicky said.

"*I'm* not being fair?" Reggie sounded outraged. "You're the one who's not fair."

"Just listen first, Reggie. Please."

Reggie pursed her lips as if to seal them. Vicky took a deep breath and pushed herself to continue. "All the years we've been friends, I respected it when you said you couldn't do something with me because you had to study. That's your thing. I'm glad you're smart. I admire you for it. But now I've got something that's important to me. You should respect that I need to spend time on it. It doesn't mean you don't matter to me anymore. I still like you best."

"No, you don't. You have Brenda."

"So can I only have one friend? Just you and nobody else?"

Reggie was silent. She kept her head down while they walked the whole length of the block and turned the corner. Vicky could practically hear her thinking.

"You don't understand," Reggie said finally. "It's so important to me."

"What is?"

"Well, loyalty."

"I'm loyal to you, Reggie. Are you loyal to me?"

They walked the rest of the way around the block in an even thicker silence. When they arrived back at the steps of the school, Reggie stopped. Her red cheeks were mottled, and her eyes were wet behind her glasses as she looked up at Vicky. "I don't know," she said. "I don't know." Then she trudged up the steps and into the school, leaving Vicky behind.

Vicky sighed. She couldn't guess whether her stubborn friend had it in her to admit to herself that she was jealous of Brenda and jealous of Vicky's passion for tennis. But if they were going to stay friends, Reggie had to admit it. More important, she had to overcome it.

• • • •

On Friday morning it snowed. It was only early November, but the sifting snowflakes promised an early winter. The snow didn't stick, although the cold did. Vicky rubbed her hands together to warm them while she waited for her teammates after school. She was first on the courts as usual, and to keep warm, she began practicing her serve.

"Want to borrow my gloves?" Sandi asked. She'd arrived, trailing the rest of the team behind her.

"No thanks," Vicky said. Sandi had hurt her thumb and wasn't playing this match. She was there to watch and give them support as captain. She had the hood of her parka up over her head and was wearing gloves and jeans.

"*I'd* borrow your gloves if my hands were small enough," Brenda said. "It's forty-five degrees out here. Good thing it's our last match until spring."

"Once we start playing, we'll warm up," Vicky said.

"Brenda won't," Kelly remarked as she unzipped her tennis bag.

"What do you mean by that?" Brenda asked indignantly.

"You don't move much on the court, Brenda. Well, I mean, you get to the ball mostly, but you don't look as if you're moving." Kelly offered a smile that didn't take the sting off her comment.

Brenda seemed upset by Kelly's offhand criticism. Her eyes questioned Vicky.

"You give me confidence," Vicky told her. "I feel like I've got the power on my side with you on the court."

Brenda smiled at her. "At least my partner appreciates me."

"Anything to tell us about this team, Sandi?" Bette asked. She was showing her prematch nervousness in the jittery way she kept bouncing the practice balls. She had changed her hair appointment at Sandi's request and was going to be on court one with Kelly. But she was uncomfortable playing court one.

"I hear they're good—not great, but good," Sandi said. "Be ready to run back to the baseline when they start sailing those high lobs over your heads. You may need to stand farther back from the net than usual to get them."

"I hate lobbers," Bette groaned.

"My grandmother lobs," Kelly said. "I always lose to her."

"I'll ask Finn to give us a lesson on lobbing one of these days," Sandi said. "By the way, he said to tell you all he's sorry he couldn't make it today. He's got a teachers' meeting."

"Sure, indoors—where it's warm," Bette said.

Their gym teacher's name gave them a focus for releasing their nervous tension. Each of them had a gripe about how little use he'd been to them all fall. The only one who had a good word to say for Mr. Finn was Sonja.

"Well, I didn't know I was foot-faulting until he told me," she said.

"You only step over the line when you serve on the forehand side," Brenda said.

"It's not that big a deal," Sandi said.

"Yeah, so long as nobody calls her on it," Brenda said.

"Look," Sandi said, "we've got to feel good about ourselves to win. Let's show this team just how good we are."

"Yay, team!" Bette said, and they all laughed.

Brenda set off for the second doubles court and Vicky walked with her, full of anxiety. She could be friendless after this game. Reggie had barely spoken to her since their big talk yesterday. It seemed to have finished off whatever was left of their friendship. As for Brenda, if this game went badly, that would no doubt be the end of their partnership and whatever else had been building between them. Vicky took deep breaths, the way Brenda had showed her. She had to focus on the challenge at hand—hitting the ball well.

They were halfway through the routine of their warm-up practice at net when the other team arrived. This group didn't have team shirts, just visors with their team name, The Aces, lettered on in Magic Marker. Brenda and Vicky's opponents were scrawny blond girls, one short with long hair, the other tall and short-haired. The short one kept missing during practice. The tall one hit soft, steady returns and hugged the baseline.

"Doesn't look as if we're going to have any problems," Brenda said.

Vicky hoped she was right. An easy win would put off the test of their relationship, and that suited her fine. She could use some relief from the tensions of the past few days. However, when the game started officially, the short one not only got the ball back but turned up with a wicked forehand cross-court. She and her partner had won the first game before Vicky and Brenda had had a chance to take their measure.

"So much for easy," Vicky said.

"Yeah, what do you think? Keep feeding balls to the tall one?"

"Maybe we should just try to hit winners," Vicky said.

"Maybe," Brenda agreed.

When Vicky served, Brenda was given the gift of two floaters, easy putaways that gave them the first two points of the second game. Then Vicky took the blond girls unaware by making an impossible return from outside the ad court, which they missed. Each server in turn took a game for her side until the score stood at four all. When the Aces won the next game, Brenda began to get desperate.

"Don't let them break your serve, Vicky. We don't want to lose the first set and end up having to play three sets to win. Hit hard right at the tall one. She scares easy."

Brenda followed her own advice and made three quick points in a row. Vicky made the fourth with a serve up the middle that the short girl missed. Now the score was 5–5. Vicky went to net and popped a ball over to the net person, who took advantage of her mistake. "Sorry," Vicky said to Brenda.

Brenda looked gloomy. They were down love–thirty. "We need to get to net faster," Brenda said.

Vicky tried. She charged the net and slapped at a ball that just hit the tape and rolled over. The short girl blew a raspberry at her.

Vicky laughed. "Luck counts," she said.

"It sure does," the short girl said, and smiled back.

It was fun to play against good-natured opponents, Vicky thought. Win or lose, she had relaxed enough to enjoy herself. The next serve was an easy one that Brenda drove down the middle for a win. Now the score was even at thirty all. Vicky moved in because it seemed that the balls had been coming in short, but this time the serve was right to the line and Vicky's swing sent it sailing out.

"Ad in," the server called.

Brenda eyed her. "We'd better get this one," she said, as if doom would follow if they didn't. The serve was to Brenda, who returned it well. Vicky went to net and tipped a ball back over, but the short girl got to it. Vicky crossed over to take the return because it was coming in short and she didn't think Brenda could get it. She hit it back up the alley, and the tall girl who'd been hanging back at the baseline missed. Back to deuce.

"Okay," Brenda said. "Now we get the next two points and the game. Then one more game and the first set is ours"

Vicky returned the serve cross-court, and the tall girl hit a high ball to the baseline. Brenda back-pedaled to get to it and Vicky ran back with her, but the ball landed on the line before either of them could reach it. Brenda opened her mouth to call it out. Brenda wanted it out. She wanted it so badly that Vicky could feel the vibes coming from her. But she hesitated and looked at Vicky.

"How do you call it?" the short girl asked impatiently.

"I saw it out," Brenda said. "But my partner can call it."

"So?" The short girl challenged Vicky.

Vicky took a deep breath. This was it. Lie and keep her relationship with Brenda, or answer honestly and lose it. But that wasn't a choice for her. She had been asked point-blank how she saw the ball, and she had seen it touch the line. "It looked good to me," she said. But she couldn't bear to look at Brenda's face.

CHAPTER 13

They lost the game on the next serve, which came in short. Now the score was 6–5 in the Aces' favor.

"You know how I hate losing the first set," Brenda said angrily.

"I know," Vicky said.

Brenda was serving. She rose up on the toes of her left foot and walloped the ball into the net— once, twice. Red-faced with dismay, she served from the ad court. The short girl returned the serve down the middle. Vicky got to it and made a passing shot that gave them the point. Brenda smashed a lob, but her cross-court went wide on the next shot, and Vicky blew an easy net shot. They were behind, 30–40, when a lob came down on the baseline. Brenda had backed up to take it after the bounce, but the bounce was so high she couldn't reach it. "Out. That was out, wasn't it, Vicky?" she demanded.

Vicky licked her lip. It had been good, hadn't it?

"If you're not sure, it's our point," the short girl said aggressively.

"I didn't say I wasn't sure," Brenda said. "I saw it out. Vicky?"

"Good," Vicky said with a sinking heart.

Brenda threw her racket down and complained, to the Aces' obvious amusement, "You don't even want to win." The two blondes couldn't hide their smiles. Vicky was embarrassed. Why did she have to be such a stickler for honesty? Why not let Brenda call it out if she saw it out? Why bend over backward to give their opponents the benefit of the doubt? Brenda was right to be angry with her. Vicky was disgusted with herself. And yet . . . she couldn't act any other way.

They changed sides for the second set. Suddenly something seemed to go wrong with the short girl's backhand, and the tall girl wasn't coming to net as much. Every shot Vicky made hit the back line, and to their credit, the Aces called the shots in. The set ended with a score of 6–2 in Brenda and Vicky's favor. Now there would have to be a third set.

"Okay," Brenda said. "We're going to do this."

They stopped for a drink of water. It had clouded over and the temperature had dropped another few degrees, but Brenda was red-faced and sweating and Vicky felt comfortably warm. "We've got to win this one, right?" Brenda's eyes were big with determination. She seemed to be trying to persuade Vicky.

"Will you hate me if we don't?" Vicky asked her.

"I might," Brenda said. "Anyway, if you give it away, I will."

"I won't give it away, Brenda. I promise."

It was Brenda who suddenly began falling apart in the third set. She lunged at balls and missed. She slammed balls out or into the net. Every time Vicky made a point, Brenda lost one. Still, it was as close a match as the first set. At 4–4, Brenda got her control back. Meanwhile, the tall girl seemed tired. She hung back at the baseline and let her partner play most of the shots.

The other matches were finished, Vicky noticed. There seemed to be a few people outside the chain-link fence watching their match, which was the only one still going. "Concentrate," Vicky muttered to herself, and she focused on the game again.

It was 5–4 in Brenda and Vicky's favor when the next questionable shot landed on the ad court sideline, so far from Brenda that she hadn't even begun to try for it. She signaled that the ball was out. Then she looked over at Vicky. "Out, right?" she said.

Her partner's anxious face made Vicky long to agree that the ball had indeed been out, but she had seen it land on the white of the line. She licked her lips and opened her mouth. "Good," she heard herself call.

The jubilation of the Aces was sickening. Vicky watched Brenda's face puff up and then tighten. "I'm sorry. I'm sorry, Brenda," she whispered. And she truly was. She felt like crying, but there wasn't time. They were back at deuce. Brenda took a deep breath and served.

"Ace," the short girl said as the ball whipped off the backhand corner of the service court. Again they were ahead. Vicky missed an alley shot. Brenda's serve at deuce was returned down the middle this time, and both Brenda and Vicky went for it, but they both missed.

Now the Aces had the advantage. Brenda served and double-faulted. The third set was at 5–5. Brenda looked discouraged. "We can still win it," Vicky said. "Only two games, Brenda."

Brenda shook her head.

"Brenda, we can win," Vicky insisted. She touched Brenda's arm, which was cold and damp.

"I'm beat," Brenda said. "I'm too tired to move."

"But so's the tall one," Vicky said.

Brenda sighed. "Okay. Let's go, then."

A wind had come up, and now the game was different. Vicky hit a ball that seemed to land on the back line from her perspective. The tall Ace called it out. They were down two points, and then it seemed an instant later the game was over. The Aces were ahead, 6–5. One more game and the Aces had the match. But if Brenda and Vicky could even up the game score again to make it 6–6, there would have to be a tiebreaker to determine the winner of the match.

It was Vicky's serve. Go to the short girl's backhand, or try for an ace on her forehand? She tried for the ace and missed. Double-fault! She never double-faulted. Her second serve went down the middle, and the tall girl missed. Time had suddenly stretched out painfully. They seemed to have been playing forever. At thirty all, Vicky hit a ball down the middle to the short Ace, but the girl returned it low, and though Brenda tried for it, she missed.

Now it was 30–40, set point. Sweat was running down the back of Brenda's neck, and her brown hair hung in wet strings even in the November chill. Vicky tried to serve an ace and failed. Her second serve went in. The tall girl returned a lob. Brenda went for it and hit into the net. The set was over, and they'd lost the match. The Aces jumped up and down, hugging each other in triumph.

Vicky followed Brenda to where they'd dropped their warm-up suits and racket covers. Quietly, she said, "It was a good match, Brenda. Another time we'll win." She held her breath, waiting for Brenda to say there would never be another match for them to play as partners. Guiltily, she waited for Brenda to accuse her of making them lose because of her line calls.

Brenda took a sip of water. Her eyes met Vicky's. "Yeah. We played pretty well, didn't we?" she said.

Vicky let out a great sigh of relief. "We did," she said. "You had some great shots."

"But you were the one with the great gets. I threw too many away." Brenda even managed to smile. They had lost, and Brenda was smiling!

Vicky put her arms around her partner and hugged her. "Thanks," she said huskily.

"Hey, listen," Brenda said, "if you want to try singles once in a while, that's okay, too. We're still friends, right?"

"Right," Vicky said. They slapped high fives.

"What a game that was!" Sandi said. She patted them both on the back at the same time. "You two were fantastic. I'm glad I stayed. The others said to say they were sorry they had to go. Too bad you lost, but next time . . ."

"Next time for sure," Brenda said.

Sandi laughed and waved as she ran off. Vicky turned to see that a small group of people was standing behind her, half hidden by juniper bushes—Derek and Reggie and, most surprising of all, Mom. Reggie was holding Woof's leash, and he was stretched out flat on the cold ground in a bear-rug position, his eyes half closed as if he were bored.

"What are you doing here?" Vicky asked them in amazement.

"Came to see you play," Derek said. "You didn't notice us, did you? I made Mom hang back with me so we wouldn't make you nervous. But you were really concentrating, Sis." He said it with pride.

"We lost."

"So?" he said. "You had some awesome gets. You're pretty good. So's your partner." He acknowledged Brenda with a nod.

"Hey, thanks," Brenda said. "And you're Vicky's mom?" she asked. "You've gotta be frozen standing here so long."

"I am, a little," Mom said. She was hunched into her black wool coat, and her face was pale from the cold. "But it was worth watching."

"Yeah, Vicky's really good on a tennis court, isn't she?" Brenda said.

"I don't know," Mom said. "I don't understand

tennis. But Vicky was beautiful, so graceful the way she flew around the court." She looked at her daughter wonderingly, as if she'd never quite seen her before.

To hide the quick tears that came to her eyes, Vicky turned to Reggie and said, "Your nose is redder even than your cheeks."

"Yeah," Reggie said. "Next time I'm going to bring some hot bricks and a folding chair."

"This is the last match," Vicky said.

"You mean forever?"

"No. Until spring."

"Yeah, well, it should be warmer then," Reggie said. "Maybe I won't need the bricks . . . I liked watching you play, Vicky. You put your whole self into it. I was thinking, 'Wow, she's my friend.'"

She looked down at her dog. "And can you believe how good Woof's been? I was afraid he'd make a fuss and want to chase the balls, but he just watched."

Vicky couldn't help it. Her tears brimmed over, and she gave up trying to hide her emotion. She threw her arms around Reggie first, and then her mother.

"Group hug time, ladies," Derek said. Grinning hugely, he managed to get his arms around all three of them by squeezing tightly.

"Hey what about me?" Brenda said. Awkwardly, they made room in their circle for her.

"Oh, you guys!" Vicky said. "I'm so glad you came." She didn't even complain when Woof got in on the act and slobbered a kiss on her cheek.

"Next time we're going to watch you win," Derek said, as if she needed encouragement.

Vicky laughed. "I already have won," she said. "It's so great having you all here. I mean . . ." And then she choked up and couldn't say another word.

Derek cocked an eyebrow at her as if he didn't understand. Brenda was looking at her as if she were crazy. Mom had a puzzled frown, but Reggie smiled and nodded. Standing there, warmed by their nearness and affection, Vicky felt the blood rush of triumph. No doubt about it. She was a winner.